GROOSHAM GRANGE

ANTHONY HOROWITZ

GROOSHAM GRANGE

PHILOMEL BOOKS

PHILOMEL BOOKS
A division of Penguin Young Readers Group.
Published by The Penguin Group.
Penguin Group (USA) Inc., 375 Hudson Street, New York, NY 10014, U.S.A.
Penguin Group (Canada), 90 Eglinton Avenue East, Suite 700, Toronto,
Ontario M4P 2Y3, Canada (a division of Pearson Penguin Canada Inc.).
Penguin Books Ltd, 80 Strand, London WC2R 0RL, England.
Penguin Ireland, 25 St. Stephen's Green, Dublin 2, Ireland
(a division of Penguin Books Ltd.).
Penguin Group (Australia), 250 Camberwell Road, Camberwell, Victoria 3124,
Australia (a division of Pearson Australia Group Pty Ltd).
Penguin Books India Pvt Ltd, 11 Community Centre, Panchsheel Park,
New Delhi – 110 017, India.
Penguin Group (NZ), 67 Apollo Drive, Rosedale, North Shore 0632,
New Zealand (a division of Pearson New Zealand Ltd).
Penguin Books (South Africa) (Pty) Ltd, 24 Sturdee Avenue, Rosebank,
Johannesburg 2196, South Africa.
Penguin Books Ltd, Registered Offices: 80 Strand, London WC2R 0RL, England.

First published in Great Britain by Methuen Children's Books, 1988.

Published simultaneously in Canada. Printed in the United States of America.
Design by Katrina Damkoehler.
Library of Congress Cataloging-in-Publication Data is available upon request.
ISBN 978-0-399-25061-3
10 9 8 7 6 5 4 3 2 1

For Nicholas and Cassian

Contents

It was dinnertime at 3 Wiernotta Mews.

Mr. and Mrs. Eliot were sitting at the dinner table with their only son, David. The meal that night had begun with a large plate of raw cabbage with cheese sauce because Mr. and Mrs. Eliot never ate meat. The atmosphere in the room was distinctly chilly. That afternoon, the last day of the Christmas term, David had brought home his report card. It had not made pleasant reading.

"Eliot has not made progress," the math teacher had written. "He can't divide or multiply and will, I fear, add up to very little."

"Woodwork?" the carpentry teacher had written. "I wish he would work!"

"If he stayed awake in class, it would be a miracle," the religion teacher had complained.

"Very poor form," the form master had concluded.

"He'll never get ahead," the headmaster had agreed.

Mr. Eliot had read all these comments with growing anger. First his face had gone red. Then his fingers had gone white. The veins in his neck had gone blue and his tongue had gone black. Mrs. Eliot had been unsure whether to call a doctor or take a color photograph, but in the end, and after several glasses of whiskey, he had calmed down.

"When I was a boy," he moaned, "if my report cards weren't first class, my father would lock me in a cupboard for a week without food. Once he chained me behind the car and drove up the thruway and that was only because I got an A-minus in Latin."

"Where did we go wrong?" Mrs. Eliot sobbed, pulling at her mauve-tinted hair. "What will the neighbors say if they find out? They'll laugh at me! I'm ruined!"

"My father would have killed me if I'd had a report card like this," Mr. Eliot continued. "He'd have tied me down to the tracks and waited for the eleven-oh-five from Charing Cross . . ."

"We could always pretend we don't have a son," Mrs. Eliot wailed. "We could say he's got a rare disease. We could say he fell off a cliff."

As you will have gathered from all this, Mr. and Mrs. Eliot were not the best sort of parents you could hope to have. Edward Eliot was a small, fat, bald man with a bristling mustache and a wart on his neck. He was the head of a bank in the financial district of London. Eileen Eliot was about a foot taller than her husband, very thin with porcelain teeth and false eyelashes. The Eliots had been married for twenty-nine years and had seven children. David's six elder sisters had all left home. Three of them had married. Three of them had emigrated to New Zealand.

David had been sitting at the far end of the polished walnut table, eating a polished walnut, which was all he had been given. He was short for his age and also rather thin—this was probably the result of being brought up on a vegetarian diet without really liking vegetables. He had brown hair, green-blue eyes, and freckles. David would have described himself as small and ugly. Girls found him cute, which in his mind was even worse.

For the last half hour his parents had been talking as if he wasn't there. But as his mother served up the main course—leek and asparagus pie with grated carrot gravy—his father turned and stared at him with a twitching eye.

"David," he said. "Your mother and I have discussed your grades and we are not pleased."

"We are not!" Mrs. Eliot agreed, bursting into tears.

"And I have decided that something must be done. I tell you now, if your grandfather were still alive, he'd have hung you upside down by your feet in the refrigerator. That's what he used to do to me if I so much as sneezed without asking permission! But I have decided to be a little less severe."

"That's right! Your father's an angel!" Mrs. Eliot sniffed into her lace handkerchief.

"I have decided, as far as you are concerned, to cancel Christmas this year. There will be no stocking, no presents, no turkey, and no snow."

"No snow?" Mrs. Eliot queried.

"Not in our garden. If any falls, I shall have it removed. I have already torn December twenty-fifth out of my calendar. This family will go from December twenty-

fourth to December twenty-sixth. However, we shall have two December twenty-sevenths to make up for it."

"I don't understand," Mrs. Eliot said.

"Don't interrupt, my precious," Mr. Eliot said, hitting her with a spoon. "If it weren't for your mother," he went on, "I would also give you a sound beating. If you ask me, there's not enough caning in this house. I was caned every day when I was a child and it never did me any harm."

"It did do you a bit of harm," Mrs. Eliot muttered in a low voice.

"Nonsense!" Mr. Eliot pushed himself away from the table in his electric wheelchair. "It made me the man I am!"

"But, darling. You can't walk . . ."

"A small price to pay for perfect manners!"

He turned the motor on and rolled toward David with a soft, wheezy noise. "Well . . . ?" he demanded. "What have you got to say?"

David took a deep breath. This was the moment he had been dreading all evening. "I can't go back," he said.

"Can't? Or won't?"

"Can't." David pulled a crumpled letter out of his pocket and handed it to his father. "I was going to tell you," he said. "I've been expelled."

"Expelled? Expelled!"

Edward Eliot sank into his wheelchair. His hand accidentally struck the controls and he shot backward into the roaring flames in the fireplace. Meanwhile Eileen Eliot, who had been about to take a sip of wine, uttered a strangled shriek and spilled the whole glass down her dress.

"I didn't like it there anyway," David said. He wouldn't normally have dared mention it. But he was in so much trouble already that a little more could hardly hurt.

"Didn't like it?" his father screamed, pouring a jug of water over himself to put out the fire.

"Beton Academy is the best private school in the country! All the best people go to Beton. Your grandfather went to Beton. Your great-grandfather went to Beton twice he liked it so much. And you can sit there and tell me . . . !"

His hand found the carving knife and he might have hurled it at his only son had Mrs. Eliot not thrown herself onto him first, taking six inches of stainless steel into her chest. "Why didn't you like it?" he rasped as she slid in a heap onto the carpet.

David swallowed. He'd already marked the door out of the corner of his eye. If things got really bad, he might have to make a dash for the bedroom. "I thought it was silly," he said. "I didn't like having to say good morning to the teachers in Latin. I didn't like cleaning other boys' boots and wearing a top hat and tails and having to eat standing on one leg just because I was under thirteen. I didn't like not having any girls there. I thought that was weird. And I didn't like all the stupid rules. When I was expelled they cut my tie in half and painted my jacket yellow in front of the whole school . . ."

"But that's tradition!" Mr. Eliot screeched. "That's what private schools are all about. I loved it at Beton. It didn't bother me that there were no girls. When I married your mother I didn't even know she was a girl. It took me ten years to find out!"

He reached down and plucked the carving knife out of Mrs. Eliot, then used it to tear open the letter. He read:

> *Dear Mr. Eliot,*
> *I very much regret to have to tell you that I have been forced to expel your son, David, for constant and willful socialism.*

Quid te exempts iuvat spinis de pluribus una?

Yours sincerely,

The Headmaster,
Beton Academy

"What does it say?" Mrs. Eliot moaned as she slowly picked herself up from the floor.

"Socialism!" In two trembling hands Mr. Eliot was holding the letter, which suddenly separated as he tore it in half, his elbow catching his wife in the eye.

"I don't want to go to private school," David said miserably. "I want to go to an ordinary school with ordinary people and—"

It was as far as he got. His father had pushed the controls of the wheelchair to fast-forward and was even now hurtling toward him with the carving knife while his mother screamed in pain. It seemed that he had just driven over her. David made a bolt for the door, reached it, and slammed it shut behind him.

"If I'd talked to my father like that, he'd have made me drink a gallon of gasoline and then . . ."

That was all he heard. He reached his bedroom and threw himself onto his bed. Downstairs he could just make out the clatter of breaking dinner plates and the muffled shouts of his parents as they blamed each other for what had happened.

It was over. It hadn't even been as bad as he had expected. But lying alone in the gloom of his bedroom, David couldn't help wondering if there wasn't going to be worse to come.

By the following morning a little sanity had returned to the Eliot household, and although David had not dared leave the safety of his bedroom yet, his parents were sitting down at the breakfast table almost as if nothing had happened.

"Are you feeling better today, my little bowl of nuts, oats, dried fruit, and whole-wheat flakes?" Mrs. Eliot inquired tenderly.

"We are not a granola," Mr. Eliot replied, helping himself to some. "How is the stab wound, my dear?"

"Not too painful, thank you, my love."

They ate their cereal in silence. As usual Mr. Eliot read the *Financial Times* from cover to cover, clicking his teeth, sniffing, and occasionally giggling as he found out which of his clients had gone bankrupt that day. On the other side of the table, Mrs. Eliot, in a bright pink bathrobe with matching hair curlers, hid behind the *Daily Mail* and slipped a little vodka into her cereal bowl. She liked a breakfast with schnapps, crackle, and pop.

It was only when they had begun eating their boiled eggs that they remembered David. Mr. Eliot had just bashed his egg with a teaspoon when his eyes glazed over and his mustache quivered.

"David . . ." he snarled.

"Do you want me to call him?" Mrs. Eliot asked.

"What are we going to do with him?" Mr. Eliot hammered at the egg again—too hard this time. The egg exploded, showering his wife with shell. With a loud sigh he threw down the spoon and tapped the *Financial Times*. "I had always hoped he would follow me into banking," he said. "That's why I bought him a pocket calculator when he was seven and a briefcase when he was eight. Every Christmas now for ten years I've been taking him to the Stock Exchange as a special treat. And what thanks have I gotten for it, eh? Expelled!" Mr. Eliot grabbed hold of the *Financial Times* and tore it into a dozen pieces. "Washed up! Finished!"

Just then there was a clatter from the hallway as the mail was delivered. Mrs. Eliot got up and went to see what had arrived, but her husband went on talking anyway.

"If only I could find a school that could lick him into shape," he muttered. "Not one of these namby-pamby modern places but somewhere that still believes in discipline. When I was young, I knew what discipline meant! These days, most children can't even spell it. Whip, whip, whip! That's what they need! A good bit of bamboo on their buns!"

Mrs. Eliot walked back into the breakfast room holding the usual bundle of bills and also a large brown envelope.

"Groosham Grange . . ." she said in a puzzled voice.

"What?"

"That's what it says on here." She held out the brown envelope. "It's postmarked Norfolk."

Mr. Eliot snatched up a knife and Mrs. Eliot dived behind the table, believing he was going to use it on her again. Instead he slit open the envelope before pulling out the contents.

"Strange . . ." he muttered.

"What is it, my dearest?" Mrs. Eliot asked nervously over the edge of the table.

"It's a prospectus . . . for a boys' school." Mr. Eliot wheeled himself closer to the window, where the sun was streaming in. "But how could anyone have known that we'd be looking for a new school for David?"

"Perhaps Beton Academy told them?" his wife suggested.

"I suppose so."

Mr. Eliot opened the prospectus and a letter slid out. He unfolded it and read out loud.

> *Dear Mr. Eliot,*
>
> *Have you ever wondered where you could find a school that could lick your son into shape? Not one of those namby-pamby modern places but some-where that still believes in discipline? And has it ever worried you that these days most children can't even spell discipline?*

Mr. Eliot lowered the letter. "Good heavens!" he said. "That's remarkable!"

"What is?" Mrs. Eliot asked.

"I was saying exactly the same thing only a moment ago! Almost word for word!"

"Go on."

Mr. Eliot picked up the letter.

Then allow us to introduce you to Groosham Grange.
As you will see from the enclosed prospectus, we are a
full boarding school and provide a unique environment
for children aged twelve to sixteen who have proved
themselves unsuited to modern teaching methods.

Groosham Grange is situated on its own island
off the coast of Norfolk. There is no regular ferry
service to the island, so there are no regular vaca-
tion days. In fact, students are permitted only one
day's vacation a year. Parents are never invited to
the school except in special circumstances—and
only if they can swim.

I feel confident that your son will benefit from
the excellent facilities and high teaching standards
of Groosham Grange. I look forward to hearing
from you in the next half hour.

Yours sincerely,

J. Kilgraw

John Kilgraw
Assistant Headmaster

"Half hour?" Mrs. Eliot said. "That doesn't give us very long to make up our minds!"

"Mine's already made up!" Mr. Eliot snapped. "Only one day's vacation a year! That's a sound idea if ever I heard one." He flicked through the prospectus, which, curiously, contained no photographs and was written in red ink on some sort of parchment. "Listen to this! They teach everything . . . with a special emphasis on chemistry, ancient history, and religious studies. They have two language laboratories, a computer room, a fully equipped gymnasium, and they're the only private school in the country with their own cemetery!" He tapped the page excitedly. "They have classes in drama, music, cooking, model making . . . and they've even got a class in astronomy."

"What would they want to have a class in a monastery for?" Mrs. Eliot asked.

"I said astronomy—the study of the stars, you ridiculous woman!" Mr. Eliot rolled up the prospectus and hit her with it. "This is the best thing that's happened all week," he went on. "Get me a telephone."

There was a number at the bottom of the letter and Mr. Eliot dialed it. There was a hiss, then a series of clicks. Mrs. Eliot sighed. Her husband always hissed and clicked when he was excited. When he was in a really good mood, he also whistled through his nose.

"Hello?" he said, once the connection had been made. "Can I speak to John Kilgraw?"

"This is Mr. Kilgraw speaking." The voice was soft, almost a whisper. "I take it this is Mr. Eliot?"

"Yes. Yes, it is. You're absolutely right!" Mr. Eliot was amazed. "I got your prospectus this morning."

"And have you come to a decision?"

"Absolutely. I wish to enroll my son as soon as possible. Between you and me, Mr. Kilgraw, David is a great disappointment to me. A massive disappointment. For many years I hoped he would follow in my footsteps—or at least in my wheelchair tracks, as I can't walk, but although he's almost thirteen, he seems totally uninterested in commercial banking."

"Don't worry, Mr. Eliot." The voice at the other end seemed to be devoid of emotion. "After a few terms at Groosham Grange I'm sure you'll find he's . . . quite a different person."

"When can he start?" Mr. Eliot asked.

"How about today?"

"Today?" Mrs. Eliot was craning her neck to listen to the receiver. Mr. Eliot swung it at her, catching her behind the ear. "I'm sorry, Mr. Kilgraw," he said as she went flying. "That was just my wife's head. Did you say today?"

"Yes. There's a train leaving Liverpool Street for King's Lynn at one o'clock this afternoon. There will be two other students on it. David could travel with them."

"That's wonderful! Do you want me to come, too?"

"Oh no, Mr. Eliot." The assistant headmaster chuckled. "We don't encourage parents here at Groosham Grange. We find our students respond more quickly if they are completely removed from home and family. Of course, if you really want to make the long and tedious journey . . ."

"No! No! I'll just put him in a taxi to the station. On second thought, make that a bus."

"Then we'll look forward to seeing him this evening. Good-bye, Mr. Eliot."

The phone went dead.

"They've accepted him!" Mr. Eliot crowed. Mrs. Eliot held the telephone out and he slammed the receiver down, accidentally crushing three of her fingers.

Just then the door opened and David came in, now wearing a T-shirt and jeans. Nervously he took his place at the table and reached out for the cereal box. At the same time his father rocketed toward him and snatched it away, sending granola in a shower over his shoulder. Mrs. Eliot had meanwhile plunged her swollen fingers into the milk. David sighed. It looked as if he was going to have to give breakfast a miss.

"You don't have time to eat," Mr. Eliot declared. "You've got to go upstairs and pack."

"Where am I going?" David asked.

"You're going to a wonderful school that I've found for you. A perfect school. A glorious school."

"But it's the end of term . . ." David began.

"The terms never end," his father replied. "That's what's so glorious about it. Pack your mother and kiss your clothes good-bye. No!" He banged his head against the table. "Kiss your mother and pack your clothes. Your train leaves at one."

David stared at his mother, who had begun to cry once again—though whether it was because he was leaving, because of the pain in her fingers, or because she had somehow managed to get her hand jammed in the milk jug he could not say. There was obviously no point in arguing. The last time he'd tried arguing, his father had locked him in his bedroom and nailed up the door. It had taken two carpenters and the fire department a week to get it open again. Silently, he got up and walked out of the room.

It didn't take him long to pack. He had no uniform for the new school and no idea what books to take. He was neither happy nor particularly sad. After all, his father had already canceled Christmas, and whatever the school was like, it could hardly be worse than Wiernotta Mews. But as he was folding his clothes, he felt something strange. He was being watched. He was sure of it.

Closing his suitcase, he walked over to the window and looked out. His bedroom had a view over the garden, which was made entirely of plastic, as his mother was allergic to flowers. And there, standing in the middle of the plastic lawn, he saw it. It was a crow, or perhaps a raven. Whatever it was, it was the biggest bird he had ever seen. It was pitch-black, its feathers hanging off it like a tattered cloak. And it was staring up at the bedroom, its glistening eyes fixed on him.

David reached down to open the window. At the same moment the bird uttered a ghastly, gurgling croak and launched itself into the air. David watched it fly away over the rooftops. Then he turned back and got ready to leave.

David arrived at Liverpool Street Station at twelve o'clock. True to his word, his father had sent him on the bus. His mother hadn't come either. She had gone into hysterics on the doorstep and Mr. Eliot had been forced to break a milk bottle over her head to calm her down. So David was quite alone as he dragged his suitcase across the courtyard and joined the line to pick up his ticket.

It was a long line—longer, in fact, than the trains everyone was waiting to get on. David had to wait more than twenty minutes before he reached a window and it was almost one o'clock before he was able to run for his train. A seat had been reserved for him—the school had arranged that—and he just had time to heave his suitcase onto the luggage rack and sit down before the whistle went and the train began to move. Pressing his face against the glass, he stared out. Slowly the train picked up speed and London shuddered and rattled away. It had begun to rain. The scene could hardly have been more gloomy if he had been sitting in a hearse on the way to his own funeral.

Half an hour later they had traveled through the suburbs and the train was speeding past a number of dreary fields—all fields look much the same when they're seen through a train window, especially when the window is covered with half an inch of dust. David hadn't time to buy himself a book or a comic book, and anyway his parents hadn't given him any money. Dejectedly, he slumped back in his seat and prepared to sit out the three-hour journey to King's Lynn.

For the first time he noticed that there were two other people in the compartment, both the same age as him, both looking as fed up as he felt. One was a boy, plump, with circular wire-framed glasses. His pants might have been the bottom of a school uniform. On top he was wearing a thick sweater made of so much wool that it looked as if the sheep might still be somewhere inside. He had long black hair that had been blown all over the place, as if he had just taken his head out of the washing machine. He was holding a half-eaten Snickers, the caramel trailing over his fingers.

The other traveler was a girl. She had a round, rather boyish face with short brown hair and blue eyes. She was quite pretty in a way, David thought, or would have been if her clothes weren't quite so peculiar. The cardigan she was wearing could have belonged to her grandmother. Her pants could have come from her brother. And wherever her coat had come from, it should have gone back immediately, as it was several sizes too big for her. She was reading a magazine. David glanced at the cover and was surprised to see that it was *Cosmopolitan*. His mother wouldn't even allow *Cosmopolitan* in the house. She said she didn't approve of "these modern women," but then, of course, his mother was virtually prehistoric.

It was the girl who broke the silence. "I'm Jill," she said.

"I'm David."

"I'm J-J-Jeffrey." It was somehow not surprising that the fat boy had a stutter.

"I suppose you're off to this Ghastly Grange?" Jill asked, folding up the magazine.

"I think it's Groosham," David told her.

"I'm sure it will be gruesome," Jill agreed. "It's my fourth school in three years and it's the only one that doesn't have any vacations."

"W-w-one day a year," Jeffrey stammered.

"W-w-one day's going to be enough for me," Jill said. "The moment I arrive, I'm heading out again."

"You'll swim away?" David asked. "It's on an island, remember."

"I'll swim all the way back to London if I have to," Jill declared.

Now that the ice had been broken, the three of them began to talk, each telling his or her own story to explain how they had ended up on a train bound for the Norfolk coast. David was first. He told them about Beton Academy, how he had been expelled, and how his parents had received the news.

"I was also at p-p-private school," Jeffrey said. "And I was expelled, too. I was c-c-caught smoking behind the football field."

"Smoking is stupid," Jill said.

"It wasn't m-m-my fault. The school bully had just set

fire to me." Jeffrey took off his glasses and wiped them on his sleeve. "I was always being b-b-bullied because I'm fat and I wear glasses and I've got a s-s-stutter."

Jeffrey's private school was called Godlesston. It was in the north of Scotland and his parents had sent him there in the hope of toughening him up. It had certainly been tough. Cold showers, twenty-mile runs, oatmeal fourteen times a week—and that was just for the staff. At Godlesston, the students had been expected to do fifty push-ups before morning chapel and twenty-one more during it. The headmaster had come to classes wearing a leopard skin and the gym teacher had bicycled to the school every day, which was all the more remarkable as he lived twenty miles away.

Poor Jeffrey had been completely unable to keep up and for him the last day of term really had been the last. The morning after he had been expelled, his father had received a prospectus from Groosham Grange. The letter that went with it had been rather different from David's. It had made the school sound like a sports complex, a massage parlor, and an army training camp all rolled into one.

"My dad also got a letter from them," Jill said. "But they told him that Groosham Grange was a really classy place. They said I'd learn table manners, and embroidery, and all that sort of stuff."

Jill's father was a diplomat, working in South America. Her mother was an actress. Neither of them was ever at home and the only time she spoke to them was on the telephone. Once her mother had bumped into her in the street and had been unable to remember who she was. But like David's parents, they were determined to give her a good education and had sent her to no fewer than three private schools.

"I ran away from the first two," she explained. "The third was a sort of finishing school in Switzerland. I had to learn flower arranging and cooking, but I was hopeless. My flowers died before I could arrange them and I gave the cooking teacher food poisoning."

"What happened then?" David asked.

"The finishing school said they were finished with me. They sent me back home. That was when the letter arrived."

Jill's father had jumped at the opportunity. Actually, he had jumped on an airplane and gone back to South America. Her mother hadn't even come home. She'd just been given two parts in a Christmas pantomime— playing both halves of the horse—and she was too busy to care. Jill's German nanny had made all the arrangements without really understanding any of them. And that was that.

By the time they had finished telling their stories, David realized that they all had one thing in common. One way or another they were "difficult" children. But even so, they had no idea what to expect at Groosham Grange. In his parents' letter it had been described as old-fashioned, and for boys only. Jeffrey's parents had been told it was some sort of educational assault course. And Jill's parents thought they were sending their daughter to a fancy ladies' academy.

"They could be three completely different places," David said. "But it's the same school."

"And there's something else p-p-peculiar," Jeffrey added. "It's meant to be on an island next to N-N-Norfolk. But I looked on the map and there are no islands. Not one."

They thought about this for a while without speaking. The train had stopped at a station and there was a bustle in the corridor as people got on and off. Then David spoke.

"Listen," he said. "However bad this Groosham Grange is, at least we're all going there together. So we ought to make a pact. We'll stick together . . . us against them."

"Like the Three M-M-Musketeers?" Jeffrey asked.

"Sort of. We won't tell anybody. It'll be like a secret society. And whatever happens, we'll always have two people we can trust."

"I'm still going to run away," Jill muttered.

"Maybe we'll go with you. At least we'll be able to help you."

"I'll lend you my swimming trunks," Jeffrey said.

Jill glanced at his bulging waist, thinking they would probably be more helpful if she used them in a parachute jump. But she kept the thought to herself. "All right," she agreed.

"Us against them."

"Us against th-th-them."

"Us against them." David held out his hand and the three of them shook.

Then the door of the compartment slid open and a young man looked in. The first thing David noticed was his dog collar—he was a vicar. The second thing was that he was holding a guitar.

"Is that free?" he asked, nodding at one of the empty seats.

"Yes." David would have preferred to have lied. The last thing he needed right now was a singing vicar. But it was obvious that they were alone.

The young man came into the compartment, beaming at them in that horrible way that very religious people sometimes do. He didn't put his guitar up on the luggage rack but leaned it against the opposite seat. He was in his thirties, with pink, rosy cheeks, fair hair, a beard, and unusually bright teeth. As well as the dog collar he was wearing a silver crucifix, a Saint Christopher medal, and a "Ban the Bomb" sign.

"I'm Father Percival," he announced, as if anybody was slightly interested in who he was. "But you can call me Jimbo." David glanced at his watch and groaned silently. There were still at least two hours to King's Lynn and already the priest was working himself up as if any moment he was going to burst into song.

"So where are you kids off to?" he demanded. "Going on vacation together? Or taking a day off?"

"We're going to s-s-school," Jeffrey told him.

"School? Fab! Triffic!" The priest looked at them and suddenly realized that none of them thought it was at all fab or triffic. "Hey—cheer up!" he exclaimed. "Life's a

35

great journey and it's first class all the way when you're traveling with Jesus."

"I thought you said your name was Jimbo," Jill muttered.

"I'll tell you what," the vicar went on, ignoring her. "I know how to cheer you youngsters up." He picked up his guitar and twanged at the strings. They were horribly out of tune. "How about a few hymns? I made this one up myself. I call it 'Jesus, You're My Buddy' and it goes like this . . ."

In the hour that followed, Jimbo played six of his own compositions, followed by "Onward Christian Soldiers," "All Things Bright and Beautiful," and, because Christmas was approaching, a dozen carols. At last he stopped and rested his guitar on his knees. David held his breath, praying that the vicar wouldn't finish off with a sermon or, worse still, pass the collection plate around the compartment. But he seemed to have exhausted himself as well as them.

"So what are your names?" he asked.

Jill told him.

"Great! That's really super. Now tell me—Dave, Jeff, and Jilly—you say you're off to school. What school's that?"

"Groosham Grange," David told him.

"Groosham Grange?" The vicar's mouth dropped open. In one second all the color had drained out of his face. His eyes bulged and one of his cheeks, no longer rosy, twitched. "Groosham Grange?" he whispered. His whole body had begun to tremble. Slowly his fair hair rippled and then stood on end.

David stared at him. The man was terrified. David had never seen anyone quite so afraid. What had he said? He had only mentioned the school's name, but now the vicar was looking at him as if he were the devil himself.

"Grrooosss . . ." The vicar tried to say the words for a third time, but they seemed to get caught on his lips and he hissed like a punctured balloon. His eyeballs were standing out like Ping-Pong balls now. His throat had gone dark mauve and it was evident from the way his body shuddered that he was no longer able to breathe.

". . . ssss." The hiss died away. The vicar's hands, suddenly claws, jerked upward, clutching at his heart. Then he collapsed, falling to the ground with a crash, a clatter, and a twang.

"Oh dear," Jill said. "I think he's dead."

The vicar had suffered a massive heart attack, but he wasn't actually dead. The guard telephoned ahead, and at King's Lynn Station a British Rail porter was standing by to whisk him away on a gurney to a waiting ambulance. David, Jill, and Jeffrey were also met. One glance at the man who was looking out for them and they would have quite happily taken the ambulance.

He was horribly deformed. If he had been involved in a dreadful car crash and then fallen into an industrial mangle, it could only have improved him. He was about five feet tall—or five feet short rather, for his head was closer to the ground than to his shoulders. This was partly due to the fact that his neck seemed to be broken, partly due to his hunched back. One of his eyes was several centimeters lower than the other and he had swollen cheeks and thin, straggly hair. He was dressed in a loose leather jacket and baggy trousers. People walking along the station were trying so hard not to look at him that one unfortunate woman accidentally fell off the platform. In truth, it was hard to look at anything else. He was holding a sign that read GROOSHAM GRANGE. With a sinking heart, David approached him, Jeffrey and Jill following behind.

"My name is Gregor," he said. His voice came out as a throaty gurgle. "Did you have a good journey?"

David had to wait for him to say this again because it sounded like, "Dit yurgh av aghoot churnik?" When he understood, he nodded, lost for words. "Bring your bags then, young masters," Gregor gurgled. "The car is outside."

The car was a hearse.

It had been repainted with the name of the school on the side, but there could be no disguising the shape, the long, flat area in the back where its grisly contents should have lain. The people in the street weren't fooled either. They stopped in respectful silence, taking off their hats as the three children were whisked away toward their new school. David wondered if he wasn't in the middle of some terrible nightmare, if he wouldn't wake up at any moment to find himself in bed at Wiernotta Mews. Cautiously, he pinched himself. It had no effect. The hunchback hooted at a van and cursed. The hearse swept through a red light.

Gregor was a most peculiar chauffeur. Because of his height and the shape of his body, he could barely see over the steering wheel. To anyone out in the street it must have looked as if the car were driving itself. It was a miracle they didn't hit anybody. David, sitting in the front seat, found himself staring at the man and blushed when Gregor turned and grinned at him.

"You're wondering how I came to look like this, young master?" he declared. "I was born like it, born all revolting. I gave my mother the heebie-jeebies, I did. Poor mother! Poor Gregor!" He wrenched at the steering wheel and they swerved to avoid a traffic island. "When I was your age, I tried to get a job in a freak show," he went on. "But they said I was overqualified. So I became the porter at Groosham Grange. I love Groosham Grange. You'll love Groosham Grange, young master. All the young masters love Groosham Grange."

They had left the city behind them now, following the coastal road up to the north. After that, David must have dozed off because the next thing he knew the sky had darkened and they seemed to be driving across the sea, the car pushing through the dark green waves. He rubbed his eyes and looked out of the window.

It wasn't the sea but a wide, flat field. The waves were grass, rippling in the wind. The field was empty, but in the distance a great windmill rose up, the white paneled wood catching the last reflections of the evening sun. He shivered. Gregor had turned the heater on in the car, but he could feel the desolation of the scene creeping in beneath the cushion of hot air.

Then he saw the sea itself. The road they were following—it was barely more than a trail—led down to a twisted wooden jetty. A boat was waiting for them, half hidden by the grass. It was an old fishing boat, held together by rust and lichen. Black smoke bubbled in the water beneath it. A pile of crates stood on the deck underneath a dirty net. A seagull circled in the air above it, sobbing quietly to itself. David hardly felt much better.

Gregor stopped the car. "We're here, young masters," he announced.

Taking their suitcases, they got out of the car and stood shivering in the breeze. David looked back at the way they had come, but after a few twists and turns the road disappeared and he realized that they could have come from anywhere. He was in a field somewhere in Norfolk with the North Sea ahead of him. But for the windmill he could have been in China for all the difference it would have made.

"Cheerful, isn't it," Jill said.

"Where are we?" David asked.

"God knows. The last town I saw was called Hunstanton, but that was half an hour ago." She pulled her cardigan around her shoulders. "I just hope we get there soon," she said.

"Why?"

"Because the sooner we arrive, the sooner I can run away."

A man had appeared, jumping down off the boat. He was wearing thigh-length boots and a fisherman's sweater. His face was almost completely hidden by a black beard, as black as the eyes that shone at them beneath a knotted mass of hair. A gold ring hung from his left ear. Give him a sword and an eye patch and he could have walked straight out of *Treasure Island*.

"You're late, Gregor," he announced.

"The traffic was bad, Captain Bloodbath."

"Well, the tide is worse. These are treacherous waters, Gregor. Treacherous tides and treacherous winds." He spat in the direction of the sea. "And I've got a treacherous wife waiting for me to get home, so let's get moving." He untied a rope at the end of the jetty. "All aboard!" he shouted. "You . . . boy! Weigh the anchor."

David did as he was told, although the anchor weighed so much that he could hardly lift it. A moment later they were away, the engine coughing, spluttering, and smoking—as indeed was Captain Bloodbath. Gregor stood beside him. The three children huddled together at the back of the boat. Jeffrey had gone an unpleasant shade of green.

"I'm not m-m-much of a sailor," he whispered.

The captain had overheard him. "Don't worry!" he chortled. "This ain't much of a boat!"

A mist had crept over the water. Now its ghostly white fingers stretched out for the boat, drawing it in. In an instant the sky had disappeared and every sound—the seagull, the engine, the chopping of the waves—seemed damp and distant. Then, as suddenly as it had come, it parted. And Skrull Island lay before them.

It was about two miles long and a mile wide with thick forest to the east. At the southern end, a cliff rose sharply out of the frothing water, chalk white at the top but a sort of muddy orange below. A twist of land jutted out of the island, curving in front of the cliff, and it was to this point that Captain Bloodbath steered the boat. Another jetty had been built here, and there was an open-top Jeep standing nearby. But there was no welcoming committee, no sign of the school.

"Stand by with the anchor!" the captain called out. Assuming he meant him, David took it. Bloodbath spun the wheel, slammed the engine into reverse, and shouted. David dropped the anchor. Jeffrey threw up over the side.

They had arrived.

"This way, young masters. Not far now. Just a little more driving." Gregor was the first on land, capering ahead. Jeffrey followed, weakly dragging his suitcase. David paused, waiting for Jill. She was watching Captain Bloodbath, who was already raising the anchor, backing the boat out.

"What are you waiting for?" he asked.

"We may need that boat one day," Jill muttered. "I wonder if he ever leaves it."

"Captain Bloodbath . . ." David shivered. "That's a funny name."

"Yes. So how come I'm not laughing?" Jill turned around and trudged along the jetty to the Jeep.

It took them five minutes to reach the school. The trail curved steeply upward, rising to the level of the cliffs, then followed the edge of the wood. Jeffrey had grabbed the front passenger seat next to Gregor. David and Jill were sitting in the back, clinging on for dear life. Every time the Jeep drove over a stone or a pothole—and there were plenty of both—they were thrown about a foot in the air, landing with a heavy bump. By the time they arrived, David knew what it must feel like to be a salad. But he quickly forgot his discomfort as he took in his first sight of Groosham Grange.

It was a huge building, taller than it was wide; a crazy mixture of battlements, barred windows, soaring towers, slanting gray slate roofs, grinning gargoyles, and ugly brick chimneys. It was as if the architects of Westminster Abbey, Victoria Station, and the Brixton gasworks had jumbled all their plans together and accidentally built the result. As the Jeep pulled up outside the front door (solid wood, studded with nails and sixteen inches thick), there was a rumble overhead and a fork of lightning crackled across the sky.

Somewhere a wolf howled.

Then the door creaked slowly open.

A woman stood in the doorway. For a moment her face was a livid blue as the lightning flashed. Then she smiled and David saw that she was, after all, human. In fact, after the peculiar horrors of Gregor and Captain Bloodbath, she seemed reassuringly normal. She was small and plump, with round cheeks and gray hair tied in a bun. Her clothes were Victorian, her high collar fastened at the neck with a silver brooch. She was about sixty years old, her skin wrinkled, her eyes twinkling behind gold half-glasses. For a moment she reminded David of his grandmother. Then he noticed the slight mustache bristling on her upper lip and decided that she reminded him of his grandfather, too.

"Hello! Hello!" she trilled as the three of them climbed down from the Jeep. "You must be David. And you're Jill and Jeffrey. Welcome to Groosham Grange!" She stood back to allow them to enter, then closed the door after them. "I'm Mrs. Windergast," she went on. "The school matron. I hope the journey hasn't been too tiring?"

"I'm tired," Gregor said.

"I wasn't asking you, you disgusting creature," the matron snapped. "I was talking to these dear, dear children." She beamed at them. "Our new arrivals!"

David looked past her, taking in his surroundings. He was in a cavernous entrance hall, all wood panels and musty oil paintings. A wider staircase swept upward, leading to a gloomy corridor. The hall was lit by a chandelier. But there were no lightbulbs. Instead, about a hundred candles spluttered and burned in brass holders, thick black smoke strangling what little light they gave.

"The others are already eating their evening meal," Mrs. Windergast said. "I do hope you like blood pudding." She beamed at them for a second time, not giving them a chance to answer. "Now—leave your suitcases here, Jeffrey and Jill. You follow me, David. Mr. Kilgraw wants to see you. It's the first door on the left."

"Why does he want to see me?" David asked.

"To welcome you, of course!" The matron seemed astonished by the question. "Mr. Kilgraw is the assistant headmaster," she went on. "He likes to welcome all his new students personally. But one at a time. I expect he'll see the others tomorrow."

Jill glanced at David and shrugged. He understood what she was trying to tell him. Mrs. Windergast might seem friendly enough, but there was an edge to her voice that suggested it would be better not to argue. He watched as Jill and Jeffrey were led away across the hall and through an archway, then went over to the door that the matron had indicated. His mouth had gone dry and he wondered why.

"I expect it's because I'm terrified," he muttered to himself.

Then he knocked on the door.

A voice called out from inside, and taking a deep breath, David opened the door and went in. He found himself in a study lined with books on one side and pictures on the other with a full-length mirror in the middle. There was something very strange about the mirror. David noticed at once, but he couldn't say exactly what it was. The glass had been cracked in one corner and the gilt frame was slightly warped. But it wasn't that. It was something else, something that made the hairs on the back of his neck stand up as if they wanted to climb out of his skin and get out of the room as fast as they could.

With an effort, he turned his eyes away. The furniture in the study was old and shabby.

There was nothing strange about that. Teachers always seemed to surround themselves with old, shabby furniture—although the dust and the cobwebs were surely taking things a bit too far. Opposite the door, in front of a red velvet curtain, a man was sitting at a desk, reading a book. As David entered, he looked up, his face expressionless.

"Please sit down," he said.

It was impossible to say how old the man was. His skin was pale and somehow ageless, like a wax model. He was dressed in a plain black suit, with a white shirt and a black tie. As David sat down in front of the desk, the man closed the book with long, bony fingers. He was incredibly thin. His movements were slow and careful. It was as if one gust of wind, one cough, or one sneeze would shatter him into a hundred pieces.

"My name is Kilgraw," he continued. "I am very happy

to see you at last, David. We are all happy that you have come to Groosham Grange."

David wasn't at all happy about it, but he said nothing.

"I congratulate you," Mr. Kilgraw went on. "The school may seem unusual to you at first glance. It may seem even . . . abnormal. But let me assure you, David, what we can teach you, what we can offer you, is beyond your wildest dreams. Are you with me?"

"Yes, sir."

Mr. Kilgraw smiled—if you could call a twitching lip and a glint of white teeth a smile. "Don't fight us, David," he said. "Try and understand us. We are different. But so are you. That is why you have been chosen. The seventh son of the seventh son. It makes you special, David. Just how special you will soon find out."

David nodded, searching for the door out of the corner of his eye. He hadn't understood anything Mr. Kilgraw had said, but it was obvious that the man was a complete nutcase. It was true that he had six elder sisters and six gruesome aunts (his father's sisters) who bought him unsuitable presents every Christmas and poked and prodded him as if he were made of Play-Doh. But how did that make him special? And in what way had he been chosen? He would never have heard of Groosham Grange if he hadn't been expelled from Beton.

"Things will become clearer to you in due course," Mr. Kilgraw said as if reading his mind. And in all probability he *had* read his mind. David would hardly have been surprised if the assistant headmaster had pulled off a mask and revealed that he came from the planet Venus. "But all that matters now is that you are here. You have arrived. You are where you were meant to be."

Mr. Kilgraw stood up and moved around the desk. There was a second, black-covered book resting at the edge and next to it an old-fashioned quill pen. Licking his fingers, he opened it, then leafed through the pages. David glanced over the top of the desk. From what he could see, the book seemed to be a list of names, written in some sort of brown ink. Mr. Kilgraw reached a blank page and picked up the quill.

"We have an old custom at Groosham Grange," he explained. "We ask our new students to sign their names in the school register. You and your two friends will bring the total up to sixty-five who are with us at present. That is five times thirteen, David. A very good number."

David had no idea why sixty-five should be any better than sixty-six or sixty-four, but he decided not to argue. Instead, he reached out for the quill. And it was then that it happened.

As David reached out, Mr. Kilgraw jerked forward. The sharp nib of the quill jabbed into David's thumb, cutting him. He cried out and shoved his thumb into his mouth.

"I'm so sorry," Mr. Kilgraw said. He didn't sound sorry at all. "Are you hurt? I can ask Mrs. Windergast to have a look at it, if you like."

"I'm all right." David was angry now. He didn't mind if Mr. Kilgraw wanted to play some sort of game with him. But he hated being treated like a baby.

"In that case, perhaps you'd be so good as to sign your name." Mr. Kilgraw held out his pen, but now it was stained bright red with David's blood. "We won't need any ink," he remarked.

David took it. He looked for ink on the desk, but there wasn't any. The assistant headmaster was leaning over him, breathing into his ear. Now all David wanted was to get out of there, to get something to eat and to go to bed. He signed his name, the nib scratching red lines across the coarse white paper.

"Excellent!" Mr. Kilgraw took the pen and slid the book around. "You can go now, David. Mrs. Windergast will be waiting for you outside."

David moved toward the door, but Mr. Kilgraw stopped him. "I do want you to be happy here, David," he said. "We at Groosham Grange have your best interests at heart. We're here to help you. And once you accept that, I promise you, you'll never look back. Believe me."

David didn't believe him, but he had no intention of arguing about it now. He went to the door as quickly as he could, forcing himself not to run. Because he had seen what was wrong with the mirror. He had seen it the moment after he had signed his name in blood, the moment he had turned away from the desk.

The mirror had reflected everything in the room. It had reflected the desk, the books, the curtains, the furniture, the carpet, and David himself.

But it hadn't reflected Mr. Kilgraw.

7:00 A.M.

Woke up with a bell jangling in my ear. The dormitory is high up in one of the school's towers. It is completely circular with the beds arranged like the numbers on the clock face. I'm at seven o'clock (which is also the time as I sit here writing this). Jeffrey is next to me at six o'clock. His pillow is on the floor, his sheets are all crumpled, and he has somehow managed to tie his blanket in a knot. No sign of Jill. The girls all sleep in another wing.

7:30 A.M.

I am now washed and dressed. One of the boys showed me the way to the bathroom. He told me his name was

William Rufus, which was a bit puzzling as I saw the name tape on his pajamas and it said James Stephens. I asked him why he was wearing somebody else's pajamas, but he just smiled as if he knew something that I didn't. I think he *does* know something I don't!

I don't think I like the boys at Groosham Grange. They're not stuck-up like everyone at Beton Academy, but they are . . . different. There was no talking after lights-out. There was no pillow fight. Nothing. At Beton Academy every new boy was given an apple-pie bed— and they used real apple pies. Here, nobody seems at all interested in me. It's as if I weren't here at all (and I wish I weren't).

7:45 A.M.

Breakfast. Eggs and bacon. But the bacon was raw and the eggs certainly didn't come out of a chicken! I have lost my appetite.

9:30 A.M.

William Rufus—if that really is his name—took me to my first class. He is short and scrawny with a turned-up nose and baby-blue eyes. He was just the sort who would always have been bullied at Beton, but I don't think there is any bullying at Groosham Grange. Everyone is too po-lite. I don't believe I just wrote that! Whoever heard of a polite schoolboy? William and I had a weird discussion on the way to the classroom.

"It's double Latin," he said.

"I hate Latin," I remarked.

I thought we'd have at least one thing in common, but I was wrong. "You'll like it here," he told me. "It's taught by Mr. Kilgraw and he's very good."

He looked at his watch. "We'd better hurry or we'll be late."

"What's the punishment for being late?" I asked.

"There are no punishments at Groosham Grange."

Good Latin teachers? A school with no punishments? Have I gone crazy?

But double Latin wasn't as bad as it sounded. At Beton Academy it was taught as a "dead" language. And the teacher wasn't much healthier. But Mr. Kilgraw spoke it fluently! So did everyone else! By the end of the class they were chatting like old friends and nobody even mentioned Caesar or the invasion of Gaul.

Another odd thing. It was a bright day, but Mr. Kilgraw taught with the shutters closed and with a candle on his desk. I asked William Rufus about this.

"He doesn't like the sun," William said. At least, I think that's what he said. He was still talking in Latin.

11:00 A.M.

Saw Jill briefly during the break. Told her about this diary. She told me about her day so far. For some reason she's in a different class than Jeffrey and me.

"I had Mr. Creer for modeling," she said.

"Pots?" I asked.

"Completely pots. We had to make figures out of wax. Men and women. And he used real hair."

Jill showed me her thumb. It was cut just like mine. She had seen Mr. Kilgraw immediately after breakfast.

"I'm seeing him after lunch," Jeffrey said.

"Bring your own ink," Jill suggested.

12:30 P.M.

English with Miss Pedicure.

Miss Pedicure must be at least a hundred years old. She is half blind and completely bald. I think she's only held together by bandages. She seems to be wrapped up in them from head to toe. I could see them poking out of her sleeves and above her collar. It took her fifteen minutes to reach her chair, and when she sat down, she almost disappeared in a cloud of dust.

Miss Pedicure does have perfect teeth. The only trouble is, she keeps them in a glass on the corner of her desk.

She taught Shakespeare. From the way she talks, you'd think she knew him personally!

1:15 P.M.

Lunch. Minced meat. But what was the animal before it was minced? I think I am going to starve to death.

3:00 P.M.

I was meant to have French this afternoon but the teacher didn't show up. I asked William Rufus why.

WILLIAM: It must be a full moon tonight. Monsieur Leloup never teaches when there's going to be a full moon.

ME: Is he sick?

WILLIAM: Well, he isn't quite himself . . .

We all had books to read, but I couldn't make heads or tails of them. I spent most of the class writing this, then examined the other kids in the room. I know most of their names now. Marion Grant—redheaded with freckles and big teeth. Bessie Dunlop—thin and pretty if you don't look too close. Roger Bacon—an Asian. Since when was Roger Bacon an Asian name?

In fact, all these names sound wrong. Bessie just doesn't look like a Bessie. Why is it that I think everyone is sharing some sort of horrible secret? And that Jeffrey, Jill, and me are the only ones on the outside?

4:30 P.M.

Soccer. We played with an inflated pig's bladder. I scored a goal, but I didn't feel too good about it. You should try heading an inflated pig's bladder . . .

6:00 P.M.

We ate the rest of the pig for supper. It was turning on a spit with an apple in its mouth. At least I managed to grab the apple!

6:30 P.M.

I am back in Monsieur Leloup's classroom doing prep. That's what I'm supposed to be doing anyway. Instead I'm writing this. And I've just noticed something. I suppose I noticed it from the very start. But it's only just now that I've realized what it is.

Everyone in the class is wearing a ring. The same ring. It is a band of plain gold with a single black stone set in the top. What on earth does it mean? I've heard of school caps and school badges, but school rings?

I have reread my first day's diary. It doesn't make a lot of sense. It's as if I've been seeing everything on a video recorder that's been fast-forwarded. I get the pieces but not the whole picture.

But if I wrote down everything, I'd end up with a

whole book. And something tells me I ought to leave time for my will.

7:30 P.M.

An hour's free time before bed. No sign of Jeffrey or Jill. Went for a walk in the fresh air.

The soccer field is at the back of the school. Next to it there's a forest—the thickest I've ever seen. It can't be very big, but the trees look like a solid wall. There's a chapel at the back and also a small cemetery.

Saw Gregor sitting on a gravestone, smoking a cigarette. "Too many of those, Gregor," I said, "and you'll be under it!" This was a joke. Gregor did not laugh.

8:15 P.M.

Happened to see Jeffrey chatting to William Rufus. The two looked like the best of friends. Is this worrying?

8:40 P.M.

In bed. The lights go out in five minutes.

I had a bath this evening. The bathroom is antique. When you turn on the tap, the water rushes out like Niagara Falls, only muddier. Got out of the bath dirtier than when I went in. Next time I'll shower.

After I'd finished writing the last entry in this diary, I put it away in the night table beside the bed with a pencil to mark the place. When I got back, the diary was in exactly the same position, but the pencil had rolled out.

SOMEBODY READ THIS WHILE I WAS OUT OF THE ROOM!

So I won't be writing any more as long as I'm at Groosham Grange. I have a feeling it would be better to keep my thoughts to myself.

Questions:

Are all the names false? If so, why?

Despite his resolution, David had learned nothing by the end of the next day. The school routine had ticked on as normal—breakfast, Latin, history, break, math, lunch, geography, soccer—except that none of it was remotely normal. It was as if everything, the classes and the books, was just an elaborate charade, and that only when it was sure that nobody was looking, the school would reveal itself in its true colors.

It was half past seven in the evening. David was working on an essay in the school library—a room that was unusual in itself in that it didn't have any books. Instead of bookshelves, the walls were lined with the heads of stuffed animals gazing out of wooden mounts with empty glass eyes. Not surprisingly, David hadn't found it very easy to concentrate on Elizabethan history with two moles, an armadillo, and a warthog staring over his shoulder.

After twenty minutes, he gave up. He had no interest in the Spanish Armada and he suspected he could say the same for Miss Pedicure (who also taught history). He examined the page he had just finished. It was more ink blots and crossing out than anything else. With a sigh he crumpled it in a ball and threw it at the wastebasket. It missed and hit the large mirror behind it. David sighed again and went over to retrieve it. But it had gone. He searched behind the wastebasket, under the chairs, and all over the carpet in front of the mirror. But the ball of paper had vanished without a trace. Suddenly, and for no good reason, David felt nervous. He glanced over his shoulder. The warthog seemed to be grinning at him. He hurried out of the library, slamming the door behind him.

A narrow, arched passageway led out from the library and back into the main hall. This was the passage he had come down on his first evening at Groosham Grange. It went past the door of Mr. Kilgraw's study, and now he paused outside it, remembering. That was when he heard the voices.

They were coming from the room opposite Mr. Kilgraw's, a room with a dark paneled door and the single word HEADS painted in gold letters. So Groosham Grange had not one but two headmasters! David filed the knowledge away, puzzled that he hadn't yet seen either of them. He quickly looked around. The other students had already left the library ahead of him. He was alone in the passage. Pretending to tie his shoelace, he knelt beside the door.

". . . settled in very well, I think." David recognized the voice at once. There could be no mistaking the dusty syllables of Mr. Kilgraw. "The girl was a touch difficult in her modeling class, but I suppose that's only to be expected."

"But they all signed?" This was a high-pitched, half-strangled voice. David could imagine someone inside the room, struggling with a tie that was tied too tight.

"There was no problem, Mr. Teagle." Mr. Kilgraw laughed, a curiously melancholy sound. "Jeffrey— the boy with the stutter—came in last. He brought his own pencil. And two bottles of ink! In the end I had to hypnotize him, I'm afraid. After that, it was easy."

"You think this Jeffrey is going to be difficult?" This

voice was the softest of the three. The second headmaster didn't speak so much as whisper.

"No, Mr. Fitch," Mr. Kilgraw replied. "If anything, he'll be the easiest. No. The one I'm worried about is Eliot."

"What's wrong with him?"

"I don't know for sure, Mr. Teagle. But he has a certain strength, an independence . . ."

"That's just what we need."

"Of course. But even so . . ."

David would have given anything to have heard more, but just then Mrs. Windergast appeared, walking toward the library. Seeing him, she stopped and blinked, her eyes flickering behind the half-glasses.

"Is there anything the matter, David?" she asked.

"No." David pointed feebly at his shoes. "I was just tying my lace."

"Very wise of you, my dear." She smiled at him. "We don't want you tripping over and breaking something, do we? But perhaps this isn't the place to do it—right outside the headmasters' study. Because somebody might think you were eavesdropping and that wouldn't be a very good impression to give in your first week, would it?"

"No," David agreed. He straightened up. "I'm sorry, Mrs. Windergast."

He moved away as quickly as he could. The matron brushed past him and went into the headmasters' study. David would have given his right arm to have heard what they were saying now. But if he was found outside the door a second time, they would probably take it.

Instead he went in search of Jeffrey and Jill. He found them outside the staff room. Jill was examining the pigeonholes, each one labeled with the name of one of the teachers.

"Have you seen Monsieur Leloup's pigeonhole?" she asked, seeing him.

"What about it?"

"It's got a pigeon in it." She pointed at it, grimacing. The bird was obviously dead. "It looks like some wild animal got it."

"What's it doing there?" David asked.

"You'll have to ask Monsieur Leloup," Jill said.

"If he ever sh-sh-shows up," Jeffrey added.

Together they walked back down the corridor. One side was lined with lockers. The other opened into classrooms. A couple of boys passed them, making their way up to the dormitories. There was almost an hour until the bell rang, but it seemed that most of the students of Groosham Grange had already gone to bed. As always, the silence in the school would have been better suited to a museum or a monastery. In the entire day, David hadn't heard a door slam or a desk bang. What was going on at Groosham Grange?

They found an empty classroom and went into it. David hadn't been in this room yet and looked around him curiously. The walls were covered with posters showing various animals—inside and out. Instead of a desk, the teacher had a long marble slab that was covered with scientific apparatus; a burner, a small metal cauldron, and various bottles of chemicals. At the far end, a white rat cowered in a cage and two toads stared unhappily out of a glass tank. The skeleton of some sort of animal stood in one corner.

"This must be the biology lab," David whispered.

"I wish it was." Jill shook her head. "All this stuff has been left out since my first class this afternoon."

"What c-c-class was that?" Jeffrey asked.

"Cooking."

David swallowed, remembering the minced meat.

Jill sat down behind one of the desks. "So let's compare notes," she said.

"Our first two days at Groosham Grange," David agreed.

"Jeffrey—you go first."

Jeffrey had little to say. He was the most miserable of the three of them, still confused after his meeting with Mr. Kilgraw. He hadn't done any work at all and had spent the whole of the last class writing a letter to his mother, begging her to take him home. The only trouble was, of course, that there was nowhere to mail it.

"I hate it here," he said. "It isn't t-t-tough like I thought it would be. But it isn't anything like I th-th-thought it would be. All the t-t-teachers are crazy. And nobody's t-t-teased me about my stammer."

"I thought you didn't like being teased," David said.

"I d-d-don't. But it would be more n-n-normal if they did."

"Nothing's normal here," Jill broke in. "First of all they make us sign our names in blood. The classes are like no classes I've ever sat through. And then there's the business of the rings."

"I saw them, too," David said.

"They're all wearing the same ring. Like some sort of bond."

"And I've found out more." David went on to describe

his discoveries of the day, starting with the mystery of the pajamas. "I may be wrong," he said, "but I get the feeling that everyone here is using false names."

"There's a boy in my class called Gideon Penman," Jill muttered.

"Exactly. What sort of a name is that?"

"B-b-but why would they have false names?" Jeffrey asked.

"And why do they want our real names in blood?" Jill added.

"I found out something about that, too," David said, and went on to describe the conversation outside the headmasters' study. He left out the bit about Jeffrey being the weakest of them mainly because he thought it would be cruel to mention it. But also because it was probably true. "All I can say is that the sooner we're out of here the better," he concluded. "There's something nasty going on at Groosham Grange. And if we stay here much longer, I think it's going to happen to us."

Jeffrey looked accusingly at Jill. "I thought you were going to r-r-run away."

"I will." Jill glanced out of the window. "But not tonight. I think there's going to be another storm."

The storm broke a few minutes later. This time there

was no lightning, but the cloudburst was spectacular nonetheless. It was as if the sea had risen up in a great tidal wave only to come crashing down on the school. At the same time, the wind whipped through it, tearing up the earth, punching into the brickwork. Loose shutters were ripped out of their frames. A gravestone exploded. A huge oak tree was snapped in half, its bare branches crashing into the soil.

It was the sound of the falling tree that woke David for the second time that day. Scrabbling in his night table, he found his flashlight and flicked it on, directing the beam at his watch. It was just after midnight. He lay back against the pillow, gazing out of the window. There was a full moon; he could just make out its shape behind the curtain of rain. When he was a child, David had never been frightened by storms. So he was surprised to find that he was trembling now.

But it wasn't the weather. In the brief moment that the flashlight had been on, he had noticed something out of the corner of his eye, something that hadn't been fully registered in his mind. Sitting up again, he turned it back on, then swung the beam across the dormitory. Then he knew what it was.

Jeffrey was asleep in the bed next to him, his head

buried underneath the covers. But otherwise the two of them were alone. When the lights had gone out at nine-thirty, the other boys in the dormitory had already been asleep. Now their beds were empty, the covers pulled back. He directed the flashlight onto their chairs. Their clothes had gone, too.

Quietly, he slipped out of bed and put on his bath-robe and slippers. Then he went to the door and opened it. There were no lights on in the school. And the silence was more profound, more frightening, than ever.

He tried a second dormitory, then a third. In each one the story was the same. The beds were empty, the clothes were gone. Outside, the rain was still falling. He could hear it pattering against the windows. He looked at his watch again, certain that he was making some sort of crazy mistake. It was twenty past twelve. So where was everybody?

He could feel his heart tugging against his chest as if it were urging him to go back to bed and forget all about it. But David was wide-awake now. He would get to the bottom of this even if it killed him. And, he thought to himself, in all probability it would.

He tiptoed down the corridor, wincing every time he stepped on a creaking floorboard. Eventually he reached a fourth dormitory. He shined the flashlight on the handle of the door.

Behind him, a hand reached out of the gloom.

It settled on his shoulder.

David felt his stomach shrink to the size of a pea. He opened his mouth to scream and only managed to stop himself by shoving the flashlight between his teeth. It was a miracle he didn't swallow it. Slowly he turned around, the back of his neck glowing bright red with the beam of the flashlight shining through his throat.

Jill stood opposite him. Like him, she was wearing a bathrobe and slippers. She looked even more frightened than he did.

"Where are they?" she whispered. "Where have they gone?"

"Nggg . . ." David remembered the flashlight in his mouth and pulled it out. "I don't know," he said. "I was trying to find out."

"I saw them go." Jill sighed, relieved to have found David awake and out of bed. "It was about twenty minutes ago. One of them woke me up as she left the dormitory. I waited a bit and then followed them."

"So where did they go?" David asked, repeating Jill's own question.

"I saw them go into the library," Jill replied. "All of them. The whole school. I listened at the door for a bit, but I couldn't hear anything, so then I went in myself. But they weren't there, David." Jill took a deep breath. David could see that she was close to tears. "They'd all vanished."

David thought back. He had been in the library after tea, surrounded by the stuffed animal heads. It was a small room, barely big enough for sixty-two people. Apart from a table, a mirror, a dozen chairs, and the animals, there was nothing in it. And that included doors. There was only one way in. Only one way back out again.

"Maybe they've all gone outside?" he suggested. "Through a window."

Jill scowled at him. "In this weather? Anyway, the windows in the library are too high. I know. I tried . . ."

"Then they must be somewhere in the school."

"No." Jill slumped against the wall, then slithered down to sit on the floor. She was exhausted—and not just from lack of sleep. "I've looked everywhere. In the classrooms, in the dining hall, in the staff room . . . everywhere. They're not here."

"They've got to be here somewhere!" David insisted. "They can't just have disappeared."

Jill made no answer. David sat down next to her and put an arm around her shoulders. Neither of them spoke. David's last words echoed in his thoughts. "They've got to be here somewhere! They can't just have disappeared."

But sitting in the dark and silent passage, he knew that he was wrong.

Impossible though it seemed, they were alone in Groosham Grange.

Skrull Island

In the Dark

Traveling
Companions

Christmas

Through
the Mirror

Expelled

Mr. Kilgraw

The Heads

A Letter

The First Day

The
Ghost Train

The Inspector

Seventh Son

The Prospectus

Escape!

Three days before Christmas it began to snow.

By Christmas Day the whole island had been blanketed out. The ground was white. The sea was white. It was difficult to tell where one ended and the other began, and standing in the fields, you felt like a single letter on a blank page in an envelope waiting to be mailed.

There was no central heating at Groosham Grange. Instead, huge logs burned in open fireplaces, crackling and hissing as if they were angry at having to share their warmth. All the windows had steamed up and the plumbing shuddered, groaned, and gurgled as the water forced its way through half-frozen pipes. A colony of bats that inhabited one of the northern towers migrated downstairs for warmth and ended up in the dining room. Nobody complained. But David found mealtimes something of a struggle with about a hundred eyes examining his rhubarb crumble upside down from the rafters.

Apart from the bats and the weather, nothing else had changed at the school. At first David had been surprised that nobody seemed to care about Christmas. Later on he had glumly accepted it. Captain Bloodbath came to the school once a week, on Tuesdays, but he never brought any letters or took any, so there were no Christmas cards. There were no Christmas decorations either. David had seen Mrs. Windergast with an armful of holly and that had raised his spirits—at least until lunchtime, when he had had his first taste of holly soup. There was no Christmas tree and, of course, no Christmas presents. Despite the snow, nobody threw any snowballs and the only snowman turned out to be Gregor, who had dozed off on his gravestone just before the heaviest fall and had to be thawed out the next day.

Only one teacher even mentioned Christmas, and this was Mr. Creer in religious studies. Mr. Creer was the only normal-looking teacher in the school. He was the youngest, too, about thirty, short with curly hair and a neat mustache. His full name was Ronald Edward Creer. David had been a little unsettled to see the same name on a tombstone in the school cemetery—"Drowned off Skrull Island: 1955–1985"—but he had assumed it was a relative. Nonetheless, Mr. Creer did smell very strongly of seaweed.

"Christmas, of course, has very little to do with Christianity." Mr. Creer gave the class a ghostly smile. All his smiles were rather ghostly. "There were festivals at the end of December long before Christianity appeared; the Roman 'Saturnalia' and the Persian 'Birth of the Sun,' for example. In the north it is a festival of the dark spirits, for it is at Christmas that the dead return from their graves."

This was all news to David. But he had to admit that living in London and being surrounded by tinsel, department-store Santas, last-minute shopping, mince pies, puddings, and too many old films on TV, Christmas had never had much to do with Christianity there either.

Christmas Day began like any other day: baths, breakfast, three classes, then lunch. For some reason, however, the classes in the afternoon had been canceled and David and Jill found themselves free to wander as they pleased. As usual, all the other students went to bed. That was what they did whenever they had any free time. Then, late at night, they would go to the library. And then they would disappear.

David and Jill had tried to follow them several times, determined to get to the bottom of the mystery, but without success. The trouble was that there was no way they could follow the others into the library without being seen, and by the time they opened the door, everyone had gone. One afternoon they searched the room thoroughly, certain that there must be a secret passage. But if there was a secret passage, it must have had a spectacularly secret entrance. All the walls seemed to be made of solid brick. A fireplace with a stone mantelpiece dominated one of them, and there was a full-length mirror in a frame decorated with bronze flowers on the other. But though David pressed and prodded all the animals while Jill fiddled with the mirror and even tried to climb up the chimney, they didn't find anything.

And where was Jeffrey during all this?

In the weeks that they had been at Groosham Grange, Jeffrey had changed, and this worried David more than anything. He still remembered Mr. Kilgraw's words. *If anything, he'll be the easiest . . .* It was certainly true that Jeffrey had taken to spending more and more time by himself and less and less time with David and Jill. Quite a few times now, David had seen him in deep conversation with William Rufus, and although he had questioned him about it, Jeffrey had refused to respond. Although there were no books in the library, he seemed to be reading a lot; old, dusty books with yellowing pages bound in cracked leather.

It was Jill, with her short temper, who had finally started an argument. She had confronted him one evening in an empty classroom as they talked about their progress—or lack of it.

"What's wrong with you?" she demanded. "You're beginning to act as if you actually like it here!"

"Perhaps I d-d-do," Jeffrey replied.

"But the whole school is crazy!"

"All p-p-private schools are crazy. But it's a lot b-b-better than Godlesston."

"But what about our promise?" David reminded him. "Us against them."

"We may be ag-g-gainst them," Jeffrey said. "But I'm not so sure that they're ag-g-gainst us."

"Then why don't you just go off and join them?" Jill snapped.

It looked as if Jeffrey had.

David and Jill were alone as they trudged across the playing fields, up to their ankles in snow. They knew every inch of the island by now. Groosham Grange was in the north. A forest sprawled all the way down to the eastern side. Its trees could have been sculpted out of stone and looked at least a thousand years old. The point, where the jetty stood, was at the southernmost end. This was a long flat area below the multicolored cliffs that soared up behind. David was sure that he could see the entrance to a cave at the bottom of the cliffs and would have liked to explore it, but there was no way they could reach it. The cliffs themselves were too sheer to climb down and the point was separated from the cave by an inlet, the waves pounding at the rocks and sharpening them into needlepoints.

There was also a river on the island—although it was more of a wide stream—running from the north into a lake beside the forest. This was where they went to now. The water had frozen over and they had thought it would be fun to go skating. But they didn't have any skates. And anyway, they didn't feel much like having fun . . . even if it was Christmas Day.

"Have you learned anything since you got here?" Jill asked.

David considered. "Not really," he admitted. "But then there are never any tests or exams or anything, so it doesn't really seem to matter."

"Well, I've learned one thing." Jill picked up a stone and threw it across the lake. It hit the ice and slithered into a tangle of weeds. "The boat comes every Tuesday. Captain Bloodbath unloads all the supplies and then he and Gregor drive up to the school. So for about one hour there's nobody on the boat."

"What of it?" David asked, suddenly interested.

"The day after Boxing Day is a Tuesday. And when they're up at the school, there is going to be somebody on the boat. Me."

"But there's nowhere to hide." David had been with Jill when she had examined the boat a week before. "We looked."

"There isn't room for two," Jill admitted. "But I figure one of us can squeeze in inside the cabin. There's a heap of old rags on the floor. I think I can hide underneath."

"So you're really going." David couldn't help feeling sad as he spoke the words. Jill was his only true friend in the school. With her gone, he would be more alone than ever.

"I've got to go, David," Jill said. "If I stay here much

longer, I'm going to go crazy . . . like Jeffrey. But once I'm away, I'll send a letter to the authorities. They'll send someone over. And I bet you anything you like, the school will be closed down a week later."

"Where will you go?" David asked.

"I've got four brothers and two sisters to choose from," Jill said. She smiled. "We were a big family. I was number seven!"

"Did your mother have brothers and sisters?" David asked.

Jill looked at him curiously. "What on earth has that got to do with anything?"

"I just wondered . . ."

"As a matter of fact, she was a number seven, too. I've got six uncles. Why do you want to know?"

"Seventh daughter of a seventh daughter," David muttered, and said no more. It meant something. It had to mean something. But what?

He was still pondering it later that evening as he sat by himself in the library. Christmas dinner—if you could call it that—had been ham and fries, the fries only slightly warmer than the ham. David was feeling really depressed for the first time since he had arrived. Jill had gone to bed early and there wasn't even any television to cheer him up. There was one television in the school, but it was a black-and-white model held together by Scotch tape. The volume switch had fallen off and the reception was so bad that the screen always resembled a miniature snowstorm. It was fine if you were watching a program about deaf-and-dumb coal miners in Siberia. Otherwise it was useless.

The door opened and he looked up. It was Jeffrey.

"Hello," he said.

"Hello, D-D-David." The fat boy stood hovering beside the door as if he was embarrassed at having been caught there.

"I haven't seen you around for a while," David said, trying to sound friendly.

"I know. I've been b-b-busy." Jeffrey looked around the room, his eyes darting behind his wire-frame spectacles. "Actually, I w-w-was looking for W-W-William."

"Your new friend?" Now David sounded scornful. "Well, he's not here. Unless of course he's under the c-c-carpet or in the f-f-fireplace or wherever it is they all go at night! And all I can say is, if you want to join them, they're welcome to you."

"I d-d-didn't . . ." Jeffrey stammered to a halt, blushing, and David felt angry with himself for having lost his temper. He opened his mouth to speak again, but at the same time Jeffrey backed out of the room, shutting the door behind him.

David got up. *He'll be the easiest.* Once again Mr. Kilgraw's words echoed in his mind. Of course Jeffrey would be the easiest of the three of them—whatever it was that Groosham Grange had planned. He was fat. He wore glasses and he had a stutter. He was one of life's victims, always the one to be bullied. And by rejecting him, David had just played right into their hands. It had been three against the rest when they began. But his own thoughtlessness had left Jeffrey out there on his own.

Quickly, he left the library. Jeffrey had already disappeared down the corridor, but David didn't mind. If he could find out what was really going on at Groosham Grange—behind the facade of the classes and everyday school life—then perhaps he might be able to put a stop to it, saving Jeffrey and himself at the same time. And he was in the perfect place to start looking. The answer had to be in one of two rooms.

He began with the door marked HEADS. In all the time he had been at the school he had never once seen the two headmasters, Mr. Fitch and Mr. Teagle. If it hadn't been for the fact that he had heard their voices, he wouldn't have believed they even existed. Now he knocked gently on the door. As he had expected, there was no reply. Glancing over his shoulder, he reached for the handle and turned it. The door opened.

David had never been in the headmasters' study before. At first sight it reminded him more of a chapel than a study. The windows were made of stained glass showing scenes from what looked like the Last Judgment, with devils prodding naked men and women into the flames. The floor was made of black marble, and there was no carpet. The bookcases, filled with ancient books like the one Jeffrey had been reading, reminded him of pews and there was even a pulpit in one corner, a carved eagle supporting a Bible on its outstretched wings.

The room had one riddle of its own. There were two headmasters at Groosham Grange. So why was there only one desk, only one chair, only one gown on the coatrack behind the door? David could find no answer to that—and no answers to anything else. The desk drawers were locked and there were no papers lying around. He spent five fruitless minutes in the study. Then he left as quietly as he had gone in.

It took more courage to sneak into Mr. Kilgraw's study

opposite. David remembered the last time he had been there—he still had a mark on his thumb to show for it. Eventually he opened the door. "He can't eat you," he muttered to himself, and wished that he believed it.

There was no sign of the assistant headmaster, but as he crossed the carpet, he felt he was being watched. He stopped, scarcely daring to breathe. He was quite alone in the room. He moved again. The eyes followed him. He stopped again. Then he realized what it was. The pictures . . . ! They were portraits of grim old men, painted, it would seem, some years after they had died. But as David moved, their eyes moved with him, so that wherever he was in the room, they were always looking at him.

He paused beside what looked like a chest of drawers and rested his hand against it. The wood vibrated underneath his fingertips. He pulled his hand away and stared at it. Had he imagined it? No—standing there alone in the study, he could hear a faint humming sound. And it was coming from the chest.

Squatting down, he reached for one of the drawers and pulled it. That was when he made his first discovery. The whole chest was a fake. All three drawers were no more than a front and swung open like a door. The chest was actually a modern refrigerator.

David peered inside and swallowed hard. The chest might be a fridge, but it certainly didn't contain milk, butter, and half a dozen eggs. Instead, about thirty plastic bags hung from hooks, each one filled with a dark red liquid. "It's wine," he whispered. "It's got to be wine. Of course it's wine. It can't be anything else. I mean, it can't be . . ."

Blood!

But even as he slammed the door and straightened up, he knew that it was. Wine didn't come in bags. Wine was never labeled AB positive. He didn't even want to ask what thirty pints of it were doing in Mr. Kilgraw's study. He didn't want to know. He just wanted to get out of the study before he ended up in another eight bags on a lower shelf.

But before he had reached the door, he managed to stop himself. It was too late to back out now. This might be the last chance he'd have to search the study. And time was running out for Jeffrey. He took a deep breath. There was nobody around. Nobody knew he was there. He had to go on.

He walked over to the desk. The book that he had signed on his first evening at the school was still in its place, and with a shaking hand he opened it. He tried to lick his thumb, but his mouth was as dry as sandpaper. His eye fell at once on the last three names: DAVID ELIOT, JILL GREEN, JEFFREY JOSEPH. Although they had faded from red to brown, they were still fresher than the names on the other pages. Leaning over the desk, he began to read.

It took him about thirty seconds to realize that there wasn't one single name in the book that he recognized. There was no William Rufus, no Bessie Dunlop or Roger Bacon. So he had been right. The other students had taken false names some time after their arrival. The only question was—why?

He closed the book. Something else had attracted his attention, lying at the far corner of the desk. It hadn't been there that first night. In fact, David had never seen one before, at least not off someone's hand. It was a ring, a special ring with a black stone set in plain gold. David reached out for it . . . and yelled. The ring was white-hot. It was as if it had just come out of the forge. It was impossible, of course. The ring had been lying there on the wooden surface ever since he had come into the room. It had to be some sort of illusion. But illusion or not, his fingers were still burned, the skin blistering.

"What are you doing here?"

David twisted around, the pain momentarily forgotten. Mr. Kilgraw was standing in the room—but that was impossible, too. The door hadn't opened. David had heard nothing. The assistant headmaster was dressed as usual in black and white as if he was on his way to a funeral. His voice had sounded curious rather than hostile, but there could be no mistaking the menace in his eyes. Clutching his hand, David desperately grappled for an excuse. Ah well, he thought to himself. Refrigerator, here I come.

"What are you doing here, David?" Mr. Kilgraw asked for a second time.

"I . . . I . . . I was looking for you, sir."

"Why?"

"Um . . ." David had a flash of inspiration. "To wish you a happy Christmas, sir."

Mr. Kilgraw's lips twitched in a faintly upwardly direction. "That's a very charming thought," he muttered in a tone of voice that actually said, "A likely story!" He gestured at David's hand. "You seem to have burned yourself."

"Yes, sir." David blushed guiltily. "I saw the ring and . . ."

Mr. Kilgraw moved forward into the room. David was careful to avoid glancing in the mirror. He knew what he would see—or rather, what he wouldn't see. He waited in silence as the assistant headmaster sat down behind the desk, wondering what would happen next.

"Sometimes it's not wise to look at things we're not meant to, David," Mr. Kilgraw said. "Especially when they're things that we don't understand." He reached out and picked up the ring. David winced, but it lay there quite coolly in the palm of his hand. "I have to say that I am very disappointed in you," Mr. Kilgraw went on. "Despite the little talk we had, it seems that you aren't making any progress at all."

"Then why don't you expel me?" David asked, surprising himself with his sudden defiance. But then there was nothing he would have liked more.

"Oh no! Nobody is ever expelled from Groosham Grange." Mr. Kilgraw chuckled to himself. "We have had difficult children in the past, but they come to accept us . . . as you will one day."

"But what do you want with me?" David couldn't contain himself any longer. "What's going on here? I know this isn't a real school. There's something horrible going on. Why won't you let me leave? I never asked to come here. Why won't you let me go and forget I ever existed? I hate it here. I hate all of you. And I'm never going to accept you, not so long as I live."

"And how long will that be?" Suddenly Mr. Kilgraw's voice was ice. Each syllable had come out as a deadly whisper. David froze, feeling the tears welling up behind his eyes. But he was certain about one thing. He wouldn't cry. Not while he was in front of Mr. Kilgraw.

But then it was as if Mr. Kilgraw relented. He threw down the ring and sat back in his chair. When he spoke again, his voice was softer.

"There is so much that you don't understand, David," he said. "But one day things will be different. Right now you'd better get that hand looked at by Mrs. Windergast."

He raised a skeletal finger to the side of his mouth, thinking for a moment in silence. "Tell her that I suggest her special ointment," he went on. "I'm sure you'll find it will give you a most . . . refreshing night's sleep."

David turned around and left the study.

It was quite late by now and as usual there was nobody around in the corridors. David made his way upstairs, deep in thought. One thing was for sure. He had no intention of visiting Mrs. Windergast. If Mr. Kilgraw was keeping fresh blood in his refrigerator, who knows what he might find in her medicine cabinet? His hand was hurting him badly. But any pain was preferable to another session with the staff of Groosham Grange.

He was therefore annoyed to find the matron waiting for him outside her office. There must have been some sort of internal telephone system in the school because she already knew what had happened to him.

"Let me have a look at your poor little hand," she trilled. "Come inside and sit down while I get a Band-Aid. We don't want it getting infected, do we? My husband got an infection—God rest his soul. All of him! It was a horrible sight at the end, I can tell you. And it only began with the teeniest scratch . . ." She ushered David into the office even as she spoke, giving him no chance to argue. "Now you sit down," she commanded, "while I open my medicine cabinet."

David sat down. The office was small and cozy with a gas fire, a colorful rug, and homemade cushions on the chairs. Embroideries hung on the wall and there were comic books scattered on a low coffee table. David took all this in while the matron busied herself at the far end, rummaging in a mirror-fronted cabinet.

As she opened it, David caught the reflection of a bird on a perch. For a moment he thought he had imagined it, but then he turned around and saw the real thing, next to the window. The bird was a black crow. At first David assumed it to be stuffed, like the animals in the library. But then it croaked and shook its wings. David shivered, remembering the crow he had seen in his garden the day he had left home.

"That's Wilfred," Mrs. Windergast explained as she sat down next to him. "Some people have goldfish. Some people have hamsters. But I've always preferred crows. My husband never liked him very much. In fact, it was Wilfred who scratched him. Sometimes he can be very naughty! Now—let's have a look at that hand."

David held out his burned hand and for the next few minutes Mrs. Windergast busied herself with antiseptic creams and Band-Aids. "There!" she exclaimed when she had finished. "That's better!"

David started to stand up, but the matron motioned at him to stay where he was.

"And tell me, my dear," she said. "How are you finding Groosham Grange?"

David was tired. He was fed up with playing games. So he told her the truth. "All the kids are weird," he said. "The staff are crazy. The island is horrible. And the school is like something out of a horror film and I wish I was back at home."

Mrs. Windergast beamed at him. "But otherwise you're perfectly happy?" she asked.

"Mrs. Windergast—"

The matron held up her hand, stopping him. "Of course I understand, my dear," she said. "It's always difficult at first. That's why I've decided to let you have a bit of my special ointment."

"What does it do?" David asked suspiciously.

"It just helps you get a good night's sleep." She had produced a tub of ointment out of her apron pocket, and before David could stop her, she unscrewed the lid and held it out to him. The ointment was thick and charcoal gray, but surprisingly it smelled kind of pleasant. It was a bitter smell, some sort of wild herb. But even the scent of it somehow relaxed him and made him feel warm inside. "Just rub it into your forehead," Mrs. Windergast coaxed him, and now her voice was soft and far away. "It'll do wonders for you, just you wait and see."

David did as he was told. He couldn't refuse. He didn't *want* to refuse. The ointment felt warm against his skin. And the moment it was on, it seemed to sink through, spreading into the flesh and all the way through to his bones.

"Now you just pop into bed, David." Was it still Mrs. Windergast talking? He could have sworn it was a different voice. "And have lots of lovely dreams."

David did dream that night.

He remembered undressing and getting into bed and then he must have been asleep except that his eyes were open and he was aware of things happening around him. The other boys in his dormitory were getting out of bed. Of course, that was no surprise. David rolled over and closed his eyes.

At least, that was what he meant to do. But the next thing he remembered, he was fully dressed and following them, walking downstairs toward the library. He stumbled at the top of the stairs and felt a hand steady him. It was William Rufus. David smiled. The other boy smiled back.

And then they were in the library. What happened

next was confusing. He was looking at himself in a mirror—the mirror that hung opposite the fireplace. But then he walked into the mirror, right into the glass. He expected it to break. But it didn't break. And then he was on the other side. He looked behind him. William Rufus tugged at his arm. He went on.

Walls of solid rock. A twisting path going deeper and deeper into the ground. The smell of salt water in the air. The dream had become fragmented now. It was as if the mirror had broken after all and he was seeing only the reflections in the shattered pieces. Now he was in some huge chamber, far underground. He could see the stalagmites, a glistening silver, soaring out of the ground, reaching up to the stalactites that hung down from above. Or was it the other way around . . . ?

A great bonfire burned in the cave, throwing fantastic shadows against the wall. The whole school had congregated there, waiting in silence for something . . . or someone. Then a man stepped out from behind a slab of natural stone. And that was one thing David could not bring himself to look at, for it was more horrible than anything he had yet seen at Groosham Grange. But later on he would remember . . .

Two headmasters, but only one desk, only one chair.

The dream disconnected in the way that dreams do. Words were spoken. Then there was a banquet, a Christmas dinner like no other he had ever had before. Meat sizzled on the open fire. Wine flowed from silver jugs. There were puddings and pastries and pies, and for the first time the students at Groosham Grange laughed and shouted and acted like they were actually alive. Music welled out of the ground and David looked for Jill. To his surprise he found her and they danced together for what seemed like hours, although he knew (because it was a dream) that it might have been only minutes.

And then finally there was a hush and everybody stood still as a single figure pressed through the crowds toward the stone slab. David wanted to call out, but he had no voice. It was Jeffrey. Mr. Kilgraw was waiting for him and he had the ring. Jeffrey was smiling, happier than David had ever seen him. He took the ring and put it on. And then, as one, the whole school began to cheer, the voices echoing against the walls, and it was with the clamor in his ears that . . . David woke up.

He had a headache and there was an unpleasant taste in his mouth. He rubbed his eyes, wondering where he was. It was morning. The cold winter sun was streaming in through the windows. Slowly, he propped himself up in bed and looked around.

And he was in bed, in his usual place in the dormitory. His clothes were just as he had left them the night before. He looked at his hand. The Band-Aid was still neatly in place. All around him, the other boys were dressing, their faces as blank as ever. David threw back the covers. It really had been no more than a dream. He half smiled to himself. Walking through mirrors? Dancing with Jill in some underground cavern? Of course it had been a dream. How could it have been anything else?

He got out of bed and stretched. He was unusually stiff this morning, as if he had just completed a twenty-mile run. He glanced to one side. Jeffrey was sitting on the bed next to him, already half dressed. David thought back to their parting in the library and sighed. He had some making up to do.

"Good morning, Jeffrey," he said.

"Good morning, David." Jeffrey sounded almost hostile.

"Look—I just wanted to say I'm sorry about yesterday. All right?"

"There's no need to apologize, David." Jeffrey pulled his shirt on. "Just forget it."

In that brief moment David noticed a lot of things.

But they all rushed in on him so quickly that he would never be quite sure which came first.

Jeffrey had changed.

He didn't just sound hostile. He *was* hostile. His voice had become as bleak and distant as all the others.

He wasn't stuttering anymore.

And the hand that was buttoning up his shirt was different, too.

It was wearing a black ring.

On Boxing Day, David sat down and wrote a letter to his father.

Groosham Grange,
Skrull Island,
Norfolk   December 26th

Dear Father,
This is a very difficult letter to write.

It was so difficult, in fact, that he tore up the first sentence three times before he was satisfied and even then he wasn't sure that he had spelled *difficult* correctly.

I know that I have always been a disappointment to you. I have never been interested
in commercial banking and I was expelled
from Beton Academy. But I now see that I was
wrong.

I have decided to get a job as a teller in
the Bank of England. If the Bank of England
won't have me, I'll try the Bank of Germany.
I'm sure you'd be proud of me if I were A Teller
the Hun.

He crossed out the last sentence, too. Then the bell
rang for lunch and it was another hour before he could
sit down and begin the next paragraph.

But there is something I have to ask you.
PLEASE TAKE ME AWAY FROM GROOSHAM
GRANGE. It's not that I don't like it here (although I don't like it at all). But it's not at all
what you were expecting. If you knew what it
was really like here, you'd never have sent me
in the first place.

I think they are involved in black magic. Mr.
Kilgraw, the assistant headmaster, is a vam-

pire. Mr. Creer, who teaches pottery, religious
studies, and math, is dead, and Miss Pedicure,
who teaches English and history, ought to be,
as she is at least six hundred years old! You'll
think I'm crazy when you read this . . .

David read it back and decided that he quite possibly
was. Could all this really be happening to him?

. . . but I promise you, I'm telling the truth.
I think they want to turn me into some sort of
zombie like they did to my friend Jeffrey. He
won't talk to me anymore. He won't even stutter to me. And I know that if I stay here much
longer, I'll be next.

David took a deep breath. His hand was aching and
he realized that he was clutching the pen so hard that it
was a miracle the ink was reaching the nib. Forcing himself to relax, he pulled the page toward him and began
again.

I can't describe all the things that have
happened to me since I got here. But I've been

stabbed, drugged, threatened, and half scared to death. I know Grandpa used to do all this to you when you were young, but I don't think it's fair when I haven't done anything wrong and I don't want to be a zombie. Please at least visit the school. Then you'll see what I mean.

I can't mail this letter to you because there's no mailbox on the island, and if you've written to me, I haven't gotten it. I'm going to give this to a friend of mine, Jill Green.

She's planning to escape tomorrow and has promised to send it to you. I've also given her your telephone number and she'll call you (reversing the charges). She'll be able to tell you everything that's happened and I just hope you believe her.

I must stop now as it's time for the afternoon class—chemistry. We're being taught the secret of life.

Help!

Your son,

David

At least nobody had come into the library while he was writing. David had been scribbling the words with one eye on the door and the other on the mirror with the result that the lines had gone all over the place and reading them again made him feel seasick. But it would have to do. He folded the page in half and then in half again. He didn't have an envelope, but Jill had promised to buy one—along with a stamp—as soon as she reached the mainland.

If all went according to plan, Captain Bloodbath would arrive at ten o'clock the following morning. Jill would skip second period and hide near the jetty. As soon as Gregor had unloaded the supplies and driven the captain up to the school, she would slip onto the boat and underneath the rags. The boat would leave at eleven. And by midday Jill would be well on her way, hitchhiking south. She had to get away. She was his only hope. But that wasn't the only worry in David's mind as he hurried along to the chemistry laboratory. She might send the letter. His father might read it. But would he believe it? Would anyone believe it?

David still wasn't sure if he believed it himself.

Jill didn't even get off the island.

She was discovered by Captain Bloodbath huddling under the rags and was jerked, trembling and miserable, back onto dry land.

"So you thought you could fool me, my pretty?" he exclaimed with a leering grin. "Thought I didn't know the waterline of my own boat? I'd know if there was an extra guppy on board. Hitch a free ride to the main-land—is that what you had in mind? Well, you'd have to sail a few high seas before you could bamboozle a Bloodbath!"

For a whole week after that, Jill waited in trepidation for something to happen to her. As David had somewhat unhelpfully told her, if you were caught trying to run away from Beton Academy, your head was shaved and you had to spend a month walking around with your shoelaces tied together. But in fact, nothing happened. There really were no punishments at Groosham Grange. If Captain Bloodbath had even bothered to mention the incident to any of the staff, they didn't take the slightest bit of notice.

And so the two of them were still there as the snow melted and the winter dripped and trickled its way toward spring. They had been on the island now for seven weeks. Nothing about the school had changed—they were still both outsiders. But David knew that he had changed. And that frightened him.

He was beginning to enjoy his life on the island. Almost despite himself, he was doing well in class. French, history, math . . . even Latin came easily to him now. He had won a spot on the varsity soccer team, and although no other school came to the island, he still enjoyed the games—even with the pig-bladder balls. And then there was Jill. David depended on her as much as she did on him. They spent all their free time together, walking and talking. And she had become the closest friend he had ever had.

So he was almost grateful that her escape had failed—
and it was that that worried him. Despite the sunshine
and the first scent of spring, something evil was going
on at Groosham Grange. And slowly, surely, it was drawing him in. If he liked it there now, how long would it be
before he became a part of it, too?

Jill kept him sane. Operation Bottle was her idea.
Every day for a week they stole whatever bottles they
could get their hands on and then threw them into the
sea with messages asking for help. They sent bottles to
their parents, to the police, to the Department of Education, and even, in one desperate moment, to the Queen.
David was fairly certain that the bottles would sink long
before they reached the coast of Norfolk or at least get
washed back up on the island. But he was wrong. One
of the bottles arrived.

It was Monsieur Leloup who announced the news.

The French teacher was a small, bald, timid-looking
man. At least, he was small, bald, and timid-looking at
the start of the month. But as the full moon approached,
he would gradually change. His body would swell out
like the Incredible Hulk, his face would become increas-
ingly ferocious, and he would develop a full head of hair.
Then, when the full moon came, he would disappear

altogether, only to appear the next day back at square one. All his clothes had been torn and stitched together so many times that he must have been surrounded by at least a mile of thread. When he got angry in class—and he did have a very short temper—he didn't shout. He barked.

He was angry that morning, the first day in February.

"It would appear zat the school 'as a leetle prob-lame," he announced in his exaggerated French accent. "The busybodies een the Department of Education 'av decide-dead to pay us a viseet. So tomorrow we must albee on our best be-evure." He glanced meaningfully at Jill and David. "And no-buddy is to speak to zis man unless 'ee speaks to them."

That evening, Jill was hardly able to contain her excitement.

"He must have gotten one of our messages," Jill said. "If the Department of Education finds out the truth about Groosham Grange, they'll close it down and that will be the end of it. We'll be free!"

"I know," David muttered gloomily. "But they won't let us anywhere near him. And if they see us talking to him, they'll probably do something terrible to him. And to us."

Jill looked at him scornfully. "Have you lost your bottle?" she demanded.

"Of course I haven't," David said. "How else do you think he got the message?"

Mr. Netherby arrived on the island the next morning. A thin, neat man in a gray suit with glasses and a leather briefcase, he was ferried over by Captain Bloodbath and met by Mr. Kilgraw. He gave them a small, official smile and a brief, official handshake and then began his official visit. He was very much the official. Wherever he went he took notes, occasionally asking questions and jotting down the answers in a neat, official hand.

To David and Jill's disgust, the whole school had put on a show for him. It was like a royal visit to a hospital when the floors are all scrubbed and the really sick patients are taken off their life-support machines and hidden away in closets. Everything that Mr. Netherby saw was designed to impress. The staff were all in their best suits and the students seemed lively, interested, and—above all—normal. He was formally introduced to a few of them and they answered his questions with just the right amount of enthusiasm. Yes, they were very happy at Groosham Grange. Yes, they were working hard. No, they had never thought of running away.

Mr. Netherby was delighted by what he saw. He couldn't fail to be. As the day wore on, he gradually unwound and even the sight of Gregor, humping a sack of potatoes down to the kitchen, only delighted him all the more.

"The City Council is very eager to find employment for disabled people," he was heard to remark. "He wouldn't by any chance be gay as well?"

"He's certainly very queer," Mr. Kilgraw concurred.

"Excellent! Excellent! First class!" Mr. Netherby nodded and checked off a page in his notebook.

By the end of the day, the inspector was in a thoroughly good mood. Although he had been sorry not to meet the heads—Mr. Kilgraw had told him that they were away at a conference—he seemed entirely satisfied by everything he had seen. David and Jill watched him in dismay. Their only chance seemed to be slipping away and there was nothing they could do about it. Mr. Kilgraw had managed things so that they had never been allowed near him. He hadn't visited any of their classes. And whenever they had drawn near him, he had been quickly steered in the opposite direction.

"It's now or never," Jill whispered as Mr. Kilgraw led his visitor toward the front door. They had just finished prep and had half an hour's free time before bed. Jill was clutching a note. She and David had written it the evening before and then carefully folded it into a square. The note read:

> THINGS ARE NOT WHAT THEY SEEM AT
> GROOSHAM GRANGE. YOU ARE IN GREAT
> DANGER. MEET US ON THE CLIFFS AT 7:45 P.M.
> DO NOT LET ANYONE ELSE SEE THIS NOTE.

Mr. Kilgraw and the inspector were walking down the corridor toward them.

"A most enjoyable day," Mr. Netherby was saying. "However, I have to tell you, Mr. Kilgraw, that my department is rather concerned that we have no record of Groosham Grange. You don't even appear to have a license."

"Is that a problem?" Mr. Kilgraw asked.

"I fear so. There'll have to be an inquiry. But I can assure you that I'll be filing a most favorable report . . ."

Jill and David knew what they had to do.

They moved at the same time, walking swiftly into the corridors as if they were hurrying to get somewhere. Halfway down they bumped into the two men who had stood aside to let them pass. At that moment David pretended to lose his balance, knocking Mr. Kilgraw back into the lockers. At the same time Jill pressed the square of paper into Mr. Netherby's hand.

"Sorry, sir," David muttered.

It had taken less than three seconds. Then they were moving away again as if nothing had happened. But the assistant headmaster hadn't seen anything. Mr. Netherby had the note. The only question was, would he turn up at the cliffs?

As soon as the two men had turned the corner, Jill and David doubled back, then left the school through a side exit that led into the cemetery. Nobody saw them go. "What's the time?" David asked.

"Quarter past seven."

"Then we've got half an hour . . . "

They ran across the playing fields, past the lake, and into the forest. It was a warm, cloudless night. The moon lit their path as they raced for the cover of the trees, but neither of them looked up, neither of them saw.

It was a full moon.

They stopped, panting, at the edge of the forest.

"Are you sure this is a good idea?" David asked.

"We've got to come this way," Jill said. "If we take the road, somebody may see us."

"But this forest gives me the creeps."

"The whole island gives me the creeps."

They pressed on through the forest. Here, with the moon shut out by a ceiling of leaves, everything was very dark and very still. It was like no forest David had ever seen. The trees seemed to be tied together in knots, thorns and briars snaking around the ancient trunks. Fantastic mushrooms bulged out of the ground only to ooze a horrible yellow when they stepped on them. Nothing stirred: not a bird, not an owl, not a breath of wind.

Then the wolf howled.

Jill seized hold of David so suddenly that she nearly tore off his shirt. "What is it?" she whispered.

"I think it was a dog," David whispered back.

"I've never heard a dog like that."

"It sounded like a dog."

"You're sure?"

"Of course I'm sure."

The wolf howled again.

They ran.

They ran whichever way they could, dodging under the low-lying branches and leaping over the undergrowth. Soon they were hopelessly lost. The forest had swallowed them up, an impossible maze that seemed to grow even as they fought their way through it. And the animal, whatever it was, was getting closer. David couldn't see it. He almost wished he could. Instead he sensed it and that was much, much worse. His imagination screamed at him. The wolf, hooking its claws into the flesh at the back of his neck. The wolf, snarling ferociously as its drooling jaws lunged at his throat. The wolf . . .

"We can't go on!" Jill almost sobbed the words, sliding to a halt.

David stopped beside her, breathless, his shirt soaked with sweat. Why had they ever decided to come this way? He had stumbled and fallen into a bed of thistles and his right hand was on fire. And their twisting path had led them into a dead end of branch and bramble. David looked around him. A heavy stick lay on the ground, blown down in one of the storms. Clutching it with both hands, he dragged it free of the nettles and picked it up.

"David . . . !"

He turned around. And now he could see something. It was too dark to tell what it was. A wolf, a man . . . or something between the two? It was just a shape, a mass of black fur with two red eyes glowing in the center. He could hear it, too. A soft, snuffling sound that made his skin crawl.

There was no way back. The creature was blocking the path.

But there was no way forward.

The creature leaped.

David swung the stick.

He had shut his eyes at the last second, but he felt the heavy piece of wood make contact. His arm shuddered. The creature screamed. Then there was a sound of the undergrowth crashing and breaking, and when he opened his eyes again, it had gone.

Jill stepped forward and laid a hand on his shoulder.

"That was no dog," she said.

"Then what was it?"

"I don't know." Jill looked thoughtfully back up the path. "But it howled with a French accent."

They had reached the southern end of the island where the land sloped steeply down, curving around to the point. Climbing through the last tangles of the forest, they crossed the road and ran to the end of the cliffs, where they had arranged to meet Mr. Netherby. Jill glanced at her watch. They had made it with ten minutes to spare.

They waited there, high up above the sea.

The top of the cliff was flat and peaceful with a soft carpet of grass. Fifty feet below, the waves glittered in the moonlight, splashing against the rocks that jutted out, looking as if they had torn through the very fabric of the sea.

"Do you think he'll come?" David asked.

"I think he's already here," Jill said.

There was somebody walking across the grass toward them, a black silhouette against the pale sky. He was still about two hundred yards away, but as he drew closer they saw that he was clutching an attaché case. Seeing them, he stopped and glanced over his shoulder. The man was afraid. They could tell simply by the way he walked.

He had covered about fifty yards, following the edge of the cliff, when it happened. At first David thought he had been stung by a wasp. But then he remembered that it was only March and there were no wasps. The man jerked, his head snapping back. One hand reached for the side of his neck. Then it happened a second time, only this time it was his shoulder. He clutched it, spinning around as if he had been shot. But there had been no gunshot. There was nobody in sight.

The man—and it was Mr. Netherby—screamed as one of his knees gave way beneath him, his voice thin and high-pitched. Then it was his back. Falling to the ground, he arched up and screamed again, both hands clawing at the air.

"What's wrong with him?" Jill whispered, her eyes wide and staring.

David shook his head, unable to speak.

It was a dreadful sight made more dreadful by the stillness of the night and the soft witness of the moon. Mr. Netherby was jerking about like an out-of-control puppet as first one part of his body, then the next, was attacked. Jill and David could only stand and watch. When it seemed that Mr. Netherby must be dead, he reached out and grabbed his attaché case, then somehow staggered to his feet. For a moment he stood there, swaying on the very edge of the cliff.

"I shall have to report this!" he called out.

Then something struck him in the heart and he toppled backward into the darkness, plummeting down to the rocks.

David and Jill said nothing for a very long time. Then David gently put his hand around her shoulders. "We'd better go back," he said.

But for David the night was not yet over.

They had slipped into the school unnoticed and whispered a trembling good night in the corridor. The other boys had already gone to bed and were sleeping as David undressed and slipped between the sheets. But he couldn't fall asleep. For what seemed like hours he lay there, thinking about what had happened and wondering what would happen next. Then he heard it.

"David . . ."

It was his own name, whispered in the darkness by someone who was not there. He turned over and buried his head in the pillow, certain that he must have imagined it.

"David . . ."

There it was again, soft, insistent, not just in his ear but inside his very head. He sat upright and looked around him. Nobody stirred.

"David, come to us . . ."

He had to obey. Almost in a trance he got out of bed, put on his bathrobe, and crept noiselessly out of the dormitory. The school was swathed in darkness, but

downstairs in the main hall he could see an open doorway with a solid rectangle of light stretching out onto
the carpet. That was where the voice wanted him to
go . . . into the staff room. He hesitated, afraid of what
he would find inside, but the voice urged him on. He
had to obey.

He walked down the staircase and, without knocking,
entered the room. There, in the harsh light, the trance
ended as David found himself face-to-face with the entire staff of Groosham Grange.

Mrs. Windergast was sitting in an armchair closest
to the door, knitting. Next to her sat Mr. Creer, his eyes
closed, scarcely breathing.

Gregor crouched beside the fireplace, muttering to
himself. Opposite the fireplace, Monsieur Leloup was also
seated, one side of his face purple and swollen. David remembered the creature in the woods, how he had beaten
it off, and he was not surprised when the French teacher
glanced at him with venom in his eyes. But it was Miss
Pedicure who drew his attention. She was sitting at a
table in the middle of the room, and as David came in
she giggled and threw something down. It was a wax
model, thin, with glasses, clutching a tiny wax attaché
case. Pins had been stuck into its neck, its arms, its legs,

and its chest, with one pin—the thirteenth—buried in its heart.

"Please come in, David."

Mr. Kilgraw was standing in front of the window with his back to the room. Now he turned around and walked back into the room, pausing at the end of the table. His eyes flickered from David to the wax doll. "Did you really think that you could fool us?" he said. There was no menace in his voice. His tone was almost matter-of-fact. But the menace was still there in the room, swirling through the air like cigarette smoke. "When you wrote that letter, you signed Mr. Netherby's death warrant. Regrettable, but you gave us no choice."

He raised his head and now his eyes settled on David.

"What are we going to do with you, David? You are doing well in your classes. You are, I think, beginning to enjoy yourself on the island. But still you resist us. We have your body. We have your mind. But you still refuse to give us your spirit."

David opened his mouth to speak, but Mr. Kilgraw silenced him with one gesture of his hand.

"We are running out of time," he said. "In fact, we have only a few days remaining. I would be sad to lose you, David. We all would. And that is why I have decided on desperate measures."

Mr. Kilgraw picked up the doll and plucked the pin out of its heart. A single drop of bright red blood dripped onto the table.

"You will report to the study at one o'clock tomorrow," he said. "I think it's time you saw the heads."

think it's time you saw the heads.

David had overheard the heads talking. He had been inside their study. But in all his time on the island he had never once seen Mr. Fitch or Mr. Teagle.

He hardly got a wink of sleep that night. Somewhere in the back of his mind he was angry. It wasn't fair. The bottles had been Jill's idea, so why had he been singled out? And what would the heads do with him when they got him? At Beton Academy any visit to the headmaster invariably meant six strokes of the cane. Even at the end-of-term sherry party he would generally cane several of the boys and even, on one memorable occasion, a couple

of the parents. And there were two headmasters at Groosham Grange. Did that mean he could expect twelve?

He finally fell asleep at about two o'clock.

It was a troubled sleep with dreams of wolves and
black rings and mirrors with no reflections. At one point
in the dream he was standing on the cliffs watching Mr.
Netherby fall. Only it was he who was holding the wax
doll, he who was jabbing the pins into it. Then his father
wheelchaired himself across the grass, waving a box of
granola, and David pointed at him and muttered something he didn't understand and his father exploded in
flames and . . .

He woke up.

The day dragged on like a sack of bricks. Math, then
history, then English literature . . . David didn't see Jill
all morning, which, in his present mood, was probably
just as well. He hardly took in a word that was said to
him. He could only think of his appointment and his
eyes were drawn to the clocks on the classroom walls.
The minute hands seemed to be moving slower than
they should have. And the other students knew. Every
now and then he caught them glancing at him. Then
they would whisper among themselves. The teachers did
their best to ignore him.

At last the time came. David was tempted to run away and hide—but he knew it would do him no good. The staff would find him and drag him out, and whatever they might think of him, he didn't want to act like a coward. At one o'clock exactly he stood outside the headmasters' study. He took a deep breath. He raised his hand. He knocked.

"Come . . ."

". . . in."

Both of them had spoken, Mr. Fitch taking the first word, Mr. Teagle the second. David went in.

The sun must have passed behind a cloud, for it was dark in the room, the light barely penetrating the stained glass windows. The black marble floor, too, made the study seem darker than it had any right to be in the middle of the day. David closed the door behind him and moved slowly toward the desk. There were two men sitting behind it, waiting for him.

No. One man.

But . . .

And then David saw with a spidery surge of horror that brushed against the bottom of his spine and scuttled all the way up to his neck. There was only one headmaster at Groosham Grange—but two heads. Or to put it another way, the heads really were heads. Mr. Fitch was quite bald with a hooked nose and vulture eyes; Mr. Teagle had thin gray hair, a tiny beard, and glasses. But the two heads were joined to one body, sitting in a dark suit and bright green tie behind the single desk in the single chair. The two heads had a neck in the shape of a letter Y. Even as David fainted, he found himself wondering which of them had chosen the tie.

He woke up back in the dormitory, lying on his own bed.

"Are you feeling better, my dear?"

Mrs. Windergast was sitting on the bed next to him, holding a sponge and a basin and watching him anxiously. She had loosened his collar and mopped his face with cold water.

"You obviously weren't quite ready to see the heads," the matron crooned on. "It can be a very upsetting experience. Poor Mr. Fitch and Mr. Teagle were both so distinguished and good-looking until their little accident."

If that was a "little" accident, David thought to himself, what would you call a major calamity?

"We're all very worried about you, David." Mrs. Windergast leaned forward with the sponge, but David reared away. It might only be water in the basin, but at

Groosham Grange you never knew. One quick slosh and you might wake up with three extra eyes and a passion for fresh blood.

The matron sighed and dropped the sponge.

"The trouble is," she said, "we've gotten to you rather late, and now we don't have much time left. How long now? Two days only! It would be such a shame to lose you, really it would. I think you're a nice boy, David. I really wish . . . !"

"Just leave me alone!" David turned his eyes away from her. He couldn't bear looking at her. Mrs. Windergast might be just like somebody's grandmother. But the somebody was probably Jack the Ripper.

"All right, dear. I can see you're still upset . . ."

Mrs. Windergast stood up and bustled out of the dormitory.

David stayed where he was, glad to be alone. He needed time to think, time to work things out. Already the memory of the headmasters had faded, as if his brain were unwilling to hold on to the image. Instead he thought about what Mrs. Windergast had just told him. *Two days only.* Why only two days?

And then it clicked. He should have realized at once.

Today was March 2. Without any vacations and with no mail arriving on the island, it was all too easy to forget the date. But March 4—in two days' time—was one day he could never forget. It was his birthday, his thirteenth birthday.

And then he remembered something else. Once, when he was talking with Jeffrey—that was when he was still able to talk with Jeffrey—the fat boy had mentioned that he was unlucky enough to have a birthday that fell on Christmas Day. In the rush of events David had managed to forget all about it, but now he remembered. It had been on Christmas Day that Jeffrey had changed. That was when he had been given his black ring. On his thirteenth birthday.

In just two days' time, David's own turn would come. Either he would accept the ring and all that came with it or . . .

But he couldn't even consider the alternative.

David swung himself off the bed and got to his feet. He couldn't wait any longer. He had no more time. He knew he had to escape from Groosham Grange. He knew when he had to go.

And suddenly he knew how.

The next day, one day before David's thirteenth birthday, Captain Bloodbath returned to the island. It was a Tuesday and he had brought with him three crates of supplies. There was to be a big party the following night—and David had no doubt that he was supposed to be the guest of honor. But he had no intention of being there. If things worked out the way he hoped, the guest of honor would be on a train to London before anyone guessed!

The sun was already setting as he and Jill crouched behind a sand dune, watching Gregor and the captain unload the last of the crates. The boat had arrived late that day. But it was there—David's last chance. He had hardly uttered a word since his encounter with the heads, and Jill, too, had been strangely silent, as if she was upset about something. But it was she who finally broke the silence.

"It's not going to work," she said. "I told you, David. There's nowhere you can hide on the boat. Not without him noticing."

"We're not going to hide on the boat," David replied.

"Well, what *are* we going to do then? Steal it?"

"Exactly."

Jill stared at him, wondering if he was joking. But David's face was pale and serious.

"Steal the boat?" she whispered.

"When we first came to the island, he left his keys in the ignition. I noticed then." David ran a dry tongue over dry lips. "It's the last thing anybody would expect. And it's our only hope."

"But do you know how to steer a boat?"

"No. But it can't be very different from a car."

"You can't drown in a car!"

David took one last quick glance back up the cliffs. Gregor and the captain had disappeared and there was no sound of the Jeep. He tapped Jill on the shoulder and they ran forward together, the pebbles crunching under their feet. The boat was bobbing up and down beside the jetty. Captain Bloodbath hadn't dropped anchor, but he had tied the boat to a post with a knot that looked like six snakes in a washing machine.

Ignoring it for the moment, David climbed on board and went over to the steering wheel, searching for the keys. The deck swayed underneath him and for a horrible moment he thought that he'd been wrong from the start—that the captain had taken the keys with him. But then the boat swayed the other way and he saw the key ring, an emerald skull, swaying at the end of a chain. The key was jutting out of the ignition. He let out a deep breath. In just a few minutes they would be gone.

"How does it work?"

Jill had gotten into the boat and was standing beside him, her voice challenging him to explain. David ran his eyes over the controls. There was a steering wheel—that was easy enough—and a lever that presumably sent the boat either backward or forward. But as for the rest of the buttons and switches, the dials and the compass, they could have been designed to send the boat on a one-way journey to the moon and David wouldn't have been any the wiser.

"So how does it work?" Jill asked again.

"It isn't difficult." David glanced at her irritably. "You just turn the key . . ."

"Then why don't you?"

"I'm going to."

He did.

Nothing happened.

David turned it again, twisting it so hard that he almost bent it in half. But still the engine refused to cough or even whimper.

"We could always swim . . ." Jill began. At the same moment David reached out and hit a large red button above the key. At once the engine chugged noisily to life, the water bubbling and smoking at the stern.

"I'll take care of the knot . . . " David began, moving away from the wheel.

"No." Jill leaned down and snatched up a fish knife that had been lying on the deck. "You stay with the controls. I'll see to the knot."

The boat was tied at the very front, and to reach the rope Jill had to climb back over the edge and onto the jetty. She stopped beside the post and set to work. It was a sharp knife but it was also a thick rope, and although she sawed back and forth with all her strength, she didn't seem to be getting anywhere. David waited for her on the boat, the wooden planks of the deck humming and vibrating beneath him. The engine seemed to be noisier than ever. Would they hear it back at the school? He looked up.

And froze.

Captain Bloodbath was coming back. The sound of the engine must have been carried up and over the cliff by the wind. Or perhaps he and Jill had been missed from dinner? Either way, the result was the same. They had been discovered and Captain Bloodbath and Gregor were speeding down the road in the Jeep, heading in their direction.

"Jill!" David called out.

But she had seen them already. "Stay where you are!" she shouted back, and redoubled her effort, sawing at the rope like a berserk violinist. By now she had cut halfway through, but Gregor and the captain were getting closer with every second that passed. Already they were approaching the bottom of the cliffs. It would take them only another twenty seconds to reach the jetty.

Jill glanced up, took a quick breath, then bent over the rope again, hacking, stabbing, and slicing with the knife. The rope was fraying now, the strands separating. But still it refused to part completely.

"Hurry!" David shouted.

There was nothing he could do. His legs had turned to stone. The Jeep reached the end of the jetty and screeched to a halt. Captain Bloodbath and Gregor leaped out. Jill's face twisted with fear, her hair blowing in the wind. But she still sawed. The knife bit into the rope. Another strand broke free.

Gregor was slightly ahead of the captain, his feet clambering down the jetty toward her. Jill cried out and sliced down the knife.

The rope broke in half.

"Jill!" David called out.

But it was too late. Gregor had leaped forward like a human toad and now he was upon her. Before Jill could move, his arms and legs were around her, dragging her to the ground.

"Go, David! Go!" she screamed.

David's hand slammed down on the lever. He felt the boat lurch underneath him as the propeller boiled the water. The boat slid out backward into the open sea, trailing the broken rope across the jetty.

Then Captain Bloodbath dived forward. With a yell of triumph his hands found the rope and clamped shut on it.

The boat was several feet out now. Jill was watching it with despairing eyes, pinned down on the jetty by the dwarf. Gregor was cackling horribly, his single eye bulging. The engine screamed. The propeller churned up white water and mud. But the boat was going nowhere. Captain Bloodbath was holding on to it, digging his heels into the wood, like a cowboy with a wild stallion. His mouth was set in a grimace. His face had gone crimson. David couldn't believe what he was seeing. The captain had to let go! He couldn't possibly stand the strain—not with the engine at full throttle.

But he hadn't pushed the reverse lever all the way down. An inch remained. With a cry of despair, David threw himself onto it, forcing it the rest of the way.

Captain Bloodbath still held on! It was an impossible tug-of-war, a man against a boat. The boat was rearing away, almost out of the water. But the man refused to let go, his hands fixed like vises on the rope . . .

"Aaaaaaargh!"

Captain Bloodbath screamed. At the same moment the boat shot backward as if catapulted.

David stared in disbelief.

The captain's hands were still clutching the rope, but they were no longer attached to his arms. The force of the engine had pulled them clean off, and as the boat rocketed away, they fell off, dropping into the sea with a faint splash like two pale crabs.

David twisted the wheel, feeling sick. The boat spun around. He jammed the lever forward. The water erupted. And then he was off, leaving Groosham Grange, Skrull Island, Jill, and a now-handless Captain Blood-bath far behind him.

David ran through the field, the grass reaching up to his armpits. Behind him the boat stood, not moored to the jetty but buried in it. The crossing had been far from smooth.

And now it was the morning of the next day. What with the mist, the currents, and the unfamiliar controls, it had taken David longer than he had thought to make the crossing and it had been dark when he had crashed into the coast of Norfolk. He had been forced to spend the night in the wrecked cabin and it was only when daylight had come that he had realized he had ended up exactly where he had begun weeks ago.

The field climbed gently up toward the brilliant white

windmill that David had first noticed from the hearse. On closer sight, the windmill turned out to be broken down and deserted, battered by the wind and the rain. The sails themselves were no more than frameworks of twisted wood, like skeleton insect wings. If David had been hoping to find a telephone there, he was disappointed. The windmill had died a hundred years ago and the telephone lines had passed it by.

But on the other side he found a main road and stood there swaying, cold and exhausted. A car sped past and he blinked. It was almost as if he had forgotten what an ordinary car looked like. He glanced nervously over his shoulder. There was no way that anybody could follow him from the school. But with Groosham Grange you never knew, and he felt lost and vulnerable out in the great silence of the plain.

He had to get to the nearest town and civilization. He had no money. That meant hitchhiking. David stretched out a hand and flicked up a thumb. Surely someone would stop. Someone had to stop.

Seventy-seven cars went by. David counted them all. Not only did they refuse to stop, but some of them actually accelerated as if anxious to avoid him. What was wrong with him? He was just an ordinary, crumpled, tired thirteen-year-old out in the middle of nowhere trying to get a lift! Thirteen! "Happy birthday!" he muttered to himself. Grimly, he stuck his thumb out and tried again.

The seventy-eighth car stopped. It was a bright red Ford Fiesta driven by a jolly, fat man called Horace Tobago. Mr. Tobago, it turned out, was a traveling salesman. As he explained, he sold practical jokes and magic tricks. Not that he needed to explain. As David sat down, his seat let out a rude noise. The candy he was offered was made of soap. And there were two doves, a rabbit, and a string of rubber sausages in the glove compartment.

"So where have you come from?" Horace asked, lifting his chin to allow his bow tie to revolve.

"From school," David muttered.

"Running away?" Horace lifted his eyebrows one at a time and wiggled his nose.

"Yes." David took a deep breath. "I have to get to a police station."

"Why?"

"I'm in danger, Mr. Tobago. The school is crazy. It's

on an island—and they're all vampires and witches and ghosts . . . and they want to turn me into one of them. I've got to stop them!"

"Ha ha ha haaargh!" Horace Tobago had a laugh like a cow being strangled. His face went bright red and the flower in his buttonhole squirted water over the dashboard. "So you're a bit of a practical joker yourself, are you, David?" he exclaimed at last. "Like a bit of a giggle? Maybe I can sell you a stink bomb or a piece of plastic puke—"

"I'm telling the truth!" David protested.

"'Course you are! 'Course you are! And my name is Count Dracula!" The joke salesman laughed again. "Vampires and witches. What a whopper, old boy! What a whopper!"

David got out of the car at the first town, Hunstanton. Mr. Tobago had laughed so much during the journey that there were tears streaming down his cheeks and a fake wart had fallen off his chin. He was still shrieking with laughter as he drove away waving, playing cards tumbling out of his sleeves. David waited until the car had gone. Then he took off.

Hunstanton was a resort town. In the summer it might have been full of color and life, but out of season it was something of a last resort, a tired jumble of gray slate roofs and towers, shops and pavilions sloping down a hillside to the edge of a cold and choppy sea. There was a quay with a cluster of fishing boats half wrapped in their own nets and looking for all the world like the fish they were meant to catch. In the distance a number of gray tents and wooden boards surrounded what might, in the summer, be an amusement park. In these sunless days of spring, there was precious little amusement to be seen anywhere.

He had to find a police station. But even as he began to search for one, he was struck by a nasty thought. Horace Tobago hadn't believed a word he had said. Why should the police? If he went in there spouting on about black magic and witchcraft, they would probably call the local asylum. Worse still, they might hold him there and call the school.

He paused and looked around him. He was standing outside a library and on an impulse he turned and went in. At least there was something he could do—find out more. The more he knew, the more he could argue his case. And books seemed the best place to start.

Unfortunately, Hunstanton Library did not have a large section on witchcraft. In fact there were only three books on the shelf and two of them had accidentally strayed out of handicrafts, which were on the shelf next door. But the third looked promising. It was called *Black Magic in Britain* by one Winny H. Zoothroat. David flicked through it, then carried it over to the table to read in more detail.

Coven: A gathering of witches, usually numbering thirteen or a multiple of thirteen. The main reason for this is that twelve is often considered a perfect number—so the figure thirteen comes to mean death. Thirteen is also the age at which a novice will be introduced.

Initiation: A new witch is often required to sign his or her name in a black book which is kept by the master of the coven. It is customary for the name to be signed in the novice's own blood. Once the novice has signed, he or she will be given a new name. This is the name of power and might be taken from a past witch as a mark of respect.

Witches: Well-known witches in Britain include Roger Bacon, who was famed for walking between two Oxford spires; Bessie Dunlop, who was burned to death in Ayrshire; and William Rufus, a thirteenth-century Master-Devil.

Sabbat: The witches' sabbath—it takes place at midnight. Before setting out for the sabbat, the witches rub an ointment of hemlock and aconite into their skin. This ointment causes a dreamlike state and, they believe, helps with the release of magical powers.

Magic: The best-known magic used by witches is called "the law of similarity." In this, a wax model stands in for the victim of the witch's anger. Whatever is done to the model, the human victim will feel.

The witch's most powerful magical tool is the familiar, a creature who acts as a sort of demonic servant. The cat is the most common sort of familiar but other animals have been used, such as pigs and even crows.

David lost track of time as he sat there reading the book. But by late afternoon, he had learned just about everything he wanted to know about Groosham Grange, as well as quite a bit that he didn't. The book had one last surprise. David was about to pick it up and return it to the shelf when it fell open on another page and his eyes lit upon an entry that leaped off the page.

Groosham Grange: *See publisher's note.*

Curiously, David turned to the end of the book. There was a brief note on the last page, written by the publisher.

> *When she was writing this book, Winny H. Zoothroat set out for the county of Norfolk to research Groosham Grange, the legendary "Academy of Witchcraft," where young novices were once taught the art of Black Magic.*
>
> *Unfortunately, Miss Zoothroat failed to return from her journey. Her typewriter was washed ashore a few months later. Out of respect to her memory, the publishers have decided to leave this section blank.*

An academy of witchcraft! The words were still buzzing in David's head as he left the library. But what else could Groosham Grange have been? Fluent Latin, wax-model making, weird cooking and very un-Christian religious studies . . . it all added up. But David had never wanted to be a witch. So why had they chosen him?

He was walking down Main Street now past the shops that were preparing to close for the day. A movement somewhere in the corner of his eye made him stop and glance back the way he had come. For a moment he thought he had imagined it. Then the same misshapen, limping figure darted out from behind a parked car.

Gregor.

Somehow the dwarf had reached Hunstanton and David knew at once that he must be looking for him. Without even thinking, he broke into a run, down the hill and out toward the sea. If he was found, he knew what would happen to him. The school would kill him rather than let him tell his story. They had already killed twice for sure. How many other people had ended up in the cemetery at Skrull Island earlier than they had expected?

It was only when he had reached the seafront that he stopped to take a breath and forced himself to calm down. It was a coincidence. It had to be. Nobody at the school could possibly know that he was still in Hunstanton.

A few feet away from him, Gregor giggled. The hunchback was sitting on a low brick wall, watching him with one beady eye. He pulled something out of his belt. It was a knife, at least seven inches long, glinting wickedly. Still giggling, he licked the blade. David turned and ran again.

He had no idea where he was going. The whole world was swaying and shuddering each time his foot thudded against the cold concrete pavement. All he could hear was his own tortured breathing. When he looked back again, the dwarf was gone. Hunstanton lay in the distance behind him. He had reached the end of the promenade.

Sagging tents and warped wooden kiosks surrounded him. The amusement park! He had wandered right into the middle of it.

"Care to take a ride, sonny?"

The speaker was an old man in a shabby coat, a cigarette dangling out of the corner of his mouth. He was standing beside the ghost train. Three carriages—blue, green, and yellow—stood on the curving track in front of the swing doors.

"A ride?" David glanced from the ghost train to the seafront. There was no sign of Gregor.

"A test run." The old man squeezed his cigarette and

coughed. "Bit of luck you showing up. You can have a free ride."

"No thanks . . ." Even as David uttered the words, Gregor appeared again, shuffling into the fairground area. He hadn't seen David yet, but he was searching. The knife was still in his hand, held low, slanting upward.

David leaped into the carriage. He had to get out of sight. A couple of minutes on a ghost train might be enough. At least Gregor couldn't follow him in there.

"Hang on tight." The old man pressed a switch.

The carriage jerked forward.

A second later it hit the doors. They broke open, then swung shut behind it. David found himself swallowed up by the darkness. He felt as if he were suffocating. Then a light glowed red behind a plastic skull and he breathed again. If the skull was meant to frighten him, it had had the opposite effect. It reminded him that this was just an entertainment, a cheap amusement-park ride with plastic masks and colored lightbulbs. A loudspeaker crackled into life with a tape-recorded "Awooo!" and David even managed a smile. A green light flicked on. A rubber spider bounced up and down on an all-too-visible wire. David smiled again.

Then the carriage plunged into a chasm.

It fell through the darkness for so long that the air rushed through David's hair and he was forced back into the seat. At the last moment, when he was sure he would be smashed to pieces at the bottom of the track, it slowed down as if hitting a cushion of air.

"Some ride . . . " he whispered to himself. It was a relief to hear the sound of his own voice.

Another light flashed on—a light that was somehow less electric than the ones that had gone before. A soft bubbling sound was coming out of the loudspeakers, only suddenly David wondered if there were any loudspeakers. It sounded too real. He could smell something, too; a damp, swamplike smell. Before the fall, he had been able to feel the tracks underneath the carriage. Now it seemed to be floating.

A figure loomed out of the darkness—a plastic model in a black cloak. But then it raised its head and David saw that it was not a model at all but a man, and a man that David knew well.

"Did you really think you could escape from us?" Mr. Kilgraw asked.

The ghost train swept forward. Mrs. Windergast stepped out in front of it. "I never thought you'd be so silly, my dear," she twittered.

David flinched as the carriage hurtled toward her, but at the last moment it was pulled aside by some invisible force and he found himself staring at Mr. Fitch and Mr. Teagle, both of them illuminated by a soft blue glow.

"A disappointment, Mr. Fitch."

"A disaster, Mr. Teagle."

The ghost train lurched backward, carrying David away. Miss Pedicure waved a finger at him and tut-tutted. Monsieur Leloup, half man, half wolf, howled. Mr. Creer, pale and semitransparent, opened his mouth to speak, but seawater flowed over his lips.

David could only sit where he was, gripping the edge of his seat, scarcely breathing as, one after another, the entire staff of Groosham Grange appeared before him. Black smoke was writhing around his feet now and he could make out a red glow in the distance, becoming brighter as he was carried toward it. Then suddenly something clanged against the back of the carriage, just above his head. He looked up. Two hands had clamped themselves against the metal, the fingers writhing. But the hands weren't attached to arms.

David yelled out.

The ghost train thundered through a second set of doors. The red glow exploded to fill his vision, a huge setting sun. A cool breeze whispered through his hair. Far below, the waves crashed against the rocks.

The ghost train had carried him back to Skrull Island. The yellow carriage was perched on the grass at the top of the cliff. There were no tracks, no models, no amusement park.

It was the evening of his thirteenth birthday and the darkness of the night was closing in.

Skrull Island

In the Dark

Traveling
Companions

Christmas

Through
the Mirror

Expelled

Mr. Kilgraw

The Heads

A Letter

The First Day

The
Ghost Train

The Inspector

Seventh Son

The Prospectus

Escape!

The school was deserted.

David had gone to bed, too depressed to do anything else. His escape had come to nothing. He had been unable to find Jill. He had just had the worst birthday of his life. And if things went the way he was expecting, it would probably also be the last.

But he couldn't sleep. Where was everybody? It had been about six o'clock when he had gotten back to the school. In four hours, lying in the dark, he had neither seen nor heard a soul. Not that there were any souls at Groosham Grange. They had all been sold long ago—and David knew who to.

A footfall on the bare wooden planks of the dormitory alerted him and he sat up, relaxing a moment later as Jill walked in.

"Jill!" He was relieved to see her.

"Hello, David." She sounded as depressed he felt. "So you didn't make it?"

"I did. But . . . well, it's a long story." David swung himself off the bed. He was still fully dressed. "Where is everybody?" he asked.

Jill shrugged. It was difficult to see her face. A veil of shadow had fallen over her eyes.

"What happened to you after I took the boat?" David asked.

"We can talk about that later," Jill replied. "Right now there's something I think I ought to show you. Come on!"

David followed her out of the dormitory, slightly puzzled by her. She looked okay enough and he assumed that nobody had punished her for her part in the escape. But she seemed cold and distant. Perhaps she blamed him for leaving her behind. David could understand that. In a way, he still blamed himself.

"I've found out a lot of things about Groosham Grange, David," she went on as they walked down the stairs. "And a lot about the staff."

"Jill . . ." David reached out to stop her. "I'm sorry I had to go without you."

"That's all right, David. It all worked out for the best." She smiled at him, but her face was pale in the gloomy half-light of the hall. Breaking away, she pressed forward, moving toward the library. "All the staff here are . . . well, they're not quite human. Mr. Kilgraw is a vampire, Mrs. Windergast is a witch. Mr. Fitch and Mr. Teagle are black magicians. They used to be two people until one of their experiments went wrong. Mr. Creer is a ghost and Miss Pedicure has lived forever."

"But what do they want with us?" David said.

"They want to teach us." Jill had reached the library door. She turned the handle and went in. "You're a seventh son of a seventh son. I'm a seventh daughter of a seventh daughter."

"What about it?"

"It means we're witches. We were born witches. It's not our fault. It's not anybody's fault, really. But like all the kids here, we have powers. The teachers just want to show us how to use them."

"Powers?" David grabbed hold of Jill and swung her around so that she faced him. She didn't resist, but her eyes seemed to look through rather than at him. "I don't have any powers. Neither do you."

"We've got them. We just don't know how to use them." Jill was standing in front of the mirror. She reached out and rapped her knuckles against the glass. Then she turned to David. "Use your power," she challenged him. "Go through the mirror."

"Through the glass?" David looked from the mirror to Jill and back again. He remembered his dream, how he had walked through the glass and into the underground cavern. But that had been just a dream. Now he was awake. The glass was solid. Only Jill, it seemed, had cracked.

"You can do it, David," she insisted. "You've got the power. All you have to do is use it!"

"But . . ."

"Try!"

Angry, confused, on the edge of fear, he wrenched himself away from her, hurling his shoulder at the glass. He would smash the mirror. That would show her. Then he would find out what was wrong with her.

His shoulder sank into the glass.

Taken by surprise, thrown off balance, David almost

stumbled. His head and his raised palms made contact with the mirror—made contact with nothing—passed through the barrier as if there were no barrier at all. It was like falling into a television set. One moment he was in the library, the next he was breathing in the cold air of the tunnel, leaning against the damp and glistening rock.

He looked back the way he had come. The tunnel seemed to end with a sheet of steel. That was what the mirror looked like from the other side. Then Jill stepped through it as if it were a sheet of water and stopped, her hands on her hips.

"You see," she said. "I told you you could do it."

"But how did you know about it?" David asked.

"I know a lot more . . ."

She brushed past him and continued down the tunnel. David followed, wondering if he was still asleep after all. But everything felt too real. He shivered in the breeze, tasted the salt water on his lips, felt the weight of the rocks hemming him in. The passage dipped down and his ears popped as the pressure increased.

"Where does this lead to?" he asked.

"You'll see."

When it seemed that they had walked half a mile, David became aware of a strange, silver glow. There had been no lightbulbs or flashlights to light the way and he realized now that the tunnel had been filled with the same silvery glow as if it were a mist rising from a subterranean lake. Jill stopped, waiting for him to catch up. He hurried forward, out of the tunnel and into . . .

It was a huge cavern, the cavern of his dream. Stalactites and stalagmites hung down, soared up, as if carved from the dreams of Nature itself. One entire wall was covered by a petrified waterfall, brilliant white, a frozen eternity. In the middle of it all stood the sacrificial block, solid granite, horribly final. Mr. Kilgraw was standing behind it. He had been waiting for them. Jill had led him to them.

David spun around, searching for something he knew he would find, something he should have seen from the start. And there it was, on her third finger. A black ring.

"Jill . . . !" He shook his head, unable to speak. "When were you thirteen?" he demanded at last.

"Yesterday," Jill said. She looked at him reproachfully. "You never wished me a happy birthday. But I don't mind, David." She smiled. "You see, we were wrong. We were fighting them. But all the time they were really on our side."

The despair was like quicksand, sucking him in. There was no more fight in him. He had failed—failed to escape, failed to do anything. Jill had been taken. She was one of them. At last he was finally alone.

And now it was his turn.

They had come for him.

As one, the students of Groosham Grange moved out of the shadows at the edge of the cavern, forming a circle around him. The rest of the staff appeared behind Mr. Kilgraw. David walked slowly to the granite block. He didn't want to walk there. But his legs would no longer obey his commands.

He stopped in front of Mr. Kilgraw. The other students had closed the circle, locking him in. Everyone was looking at him.

"You have fought us long and hard, David," Mr. Kilgraw said. "I congratulate you on your courage. But the time for fighting is over. Today is your thirteenth birthday. Midnight is approaching. You must make your choice.

"Listen to me, David. You are the seventh son of a

seventh son. That is why you were brought to Groosham Grange. You have powers. We want to teach you how to use them."

"I'm not a witch!" David cried. The words echoed around the cavern. "I never will be!"

"Why not?" Mr. Kilgraw had not raised his voice, but he was speaking with an intensity and a passion that David had never heard before. "Why not, David? Why do you refuse to see things our way? You think ghosts and witches and vampires and two-headed monsters are bad. Why? Do you know what that is, David? It's prejudice. Racial prejudice!"

Mr. Fitch and Mr. Teagle nodded appreciatively. Mrs. Windergast muttered a brief "Hear! Hear!"

"There's nothing bad about us. Have we hurt you? True, we had to see to Mr. Netherby, but that was no fault of ours. You brought him here. We were only protecting ourselves.

"The trouble is, you've seen too many horror films. We vampires have never had a fair deal on the screen. And look at werewolves! Just because my good friend Monsieur Leloup likes the occasional pigeon salad when there's a full moon, everyone thinks they've a right to hunt him down and shoot silver bullets in him. And what about Mr. Creer? All right, so he's dead. But he's still a very good teacher—in fact, he's a lot more lively than quite a few living teachers I could mention."

"But I'm not like you," David insisted. "I don't want to be like you."

"You have power," Mr. Kilgraw replied. "That is all that matters. And the real question you should be asking yourself, David, is, do you really want to stay with your parents and follow your singularly unpleasant father into commercial banking? Or do you want to be free?

"Join us, and you'll be rich. We can teach you how to make gold out of lead, how to destroy your enemies just by snapping your fingers. We can show you how to see into the future and use it for yourself. Think of it, David! You can have everything you want . . . and more. Look at Miss Pedicure! She's lived forever. So can you . . .

"All right, I admit it. We are, frankly, evil. My friends Mr. Fitch and Mr. Teagle are more evil than any of us. They've won awards for being evil. But what's so bad about being evil? *We've* never dropped an atom bomb on anyone. *We've* never polluted the environment or experimented on animals or cut back on entitlement programs for the disadvantaged. Our evil is rather agreeable. Why do you think there have been so many books and movies about us? It's because people like us. We are actually rather pleasantly evil."

While Mr. Kilgraw had spoken, the sixty-four students of Groosham Grange, novice witches and young adepts all, had tightened the circle. Now they were moving closer to David, their eyes bearing down on him. Jill was next to Jeffrey. William Rufus was on the other side. Sixty-four black rings glowed in the underground light.

Mr. Kilgraw held the sixty-fifth.

"I have enjoyed the fight, David," he said. "I didn't want it to be easy. I admire courage. But now it is midnight." He reached out with his other hand. Gregor scurried forward and gave him his knife.

"Here is your choice," he went on. "The ring or the knife? You can reject us one final time. In that case, I regret that I will be forced to plunge the blade into your heart. I can assure you that it will hurt me more than it will hurt you. And we'll give you a decent burial in the school cemetery.

"Alternatively, you can accept us, take a new name,

and begin your education in earnest. But there can be no going back, David. If you join us, you join us forever."

David felt himself being forced down onto the granite block. The circle of faces spun around him. There was the ring. And there was the knife.

"Now, David," Mr. Kilgraw asked. "What do you say?"

When I was a boy," Mr. Eliot said, "I had to work during my vacations. My father made me work so hard I'd have to spend three weeks in the hospital before I could go back to school."

"But David's only got one day's vacation," Mrs. Eliot reminded him, pouring herself a glass of gin.

"I am aware of that, my dear." Mr. Eliot snatched the glass out of her hand and drank it himself. "And if you ask me, one day is much too long. If I'd been expelled from Beton Academy, my father would never have spoken to me again. In fact, he'd have cut off my ears so I wouldn't hear him if he spoke to me accidentally."

The two parents were sitting in the living room of their

house in Wiernotta Mews. Edward Eliot was smoking a cigar. Eileen Eliot was stroking Beefeater, her favorite Siamese cat. They had just eaten lunch—ham salad served in true vegetarian style, without the ham. "Maybe we should take him to a movie or something?" Mrs. Eliot suggested nervously.

"A movie?"

"Well . . . or a concert . . ."

"Are you crazy?" Mr. Eliot snapped. He leaned forward angrily and stubbed his cigar out on the cat. The cat screeched and leaped off Mrs. Eliot, its back claws ripping off most of her stockings and part of her leg. "Why should we take him anywhere?" Mr. Eliot demanded.

"Perhaps you are right, my love," Mrs. Eliot whimpered, pouring the rest of the gin onto her leg to stop the bleeding.

Just then the door opened and David walked in.

He had changed since his departure for Groosham Grange. He was thinner, older, somehow wiser. He had always been quiet. But now there was something strange about his silence. It was like a wall between him and his parents. And when he looked at them, it was with soft, almost merciless eyes.

Mr. Eliot glanced at his watch. "Well, David," he said. "You've got seven hours and twenty-two minutes before your vacation's over. So why don't you go and mow the lawn?"

"But it's a plastic lawn!" Mrs. Eliot protested.

"Then he can go and wash it!"

"Of course, dear!" Mrs. Eliot beamed at her husband, then fainted from loss of blood.

David sighed. Seven hours and twenty-two minutes. He hadn't realized there was still so much time.

He lifted his right hand.

"What's that you're wearing?" his father demanded.

David muttered a few words under his breath.

There was no puff of smoke, no flash of light. But it was as if his parents had been photographed and at the same time turned into those photographs. Mrs. Eliot was halfway out of her chair, slumping toward the carpet. Mr. Eliot was about to speak, his mouth open, his tongue hovering over his teeth.

It was a simple spell. But they would remain that way for the next three weeks.

David rubbed his black ring thoughtfully. He had spoken the words of power with perfect pronunciation. Mrs. Windergast would have said that three weeks was overdoing it when a few hours would have been enough, but then she was a perfectionist and all David's spells tended to be on the strong side. Maybe he was just a little enthusiastic.

He went upstairs and lay down on his bed. A chocolate milk shake materialized in thin air and began to float toward him. He was looking forward to the next term at Groosham Grange. He and Jill would both be taking their first major exams in the summer: Telepathy, Weather Control, Wax Modeling, and (the trickiest of the four) Advanced Blood Sacrifice.

And what then? He sipped the milk shake and smiled. He'd gotten it exactly right—thick with plenty of chocolate. He still blushed when he remembered his first attempt. In cooking class he'd conjured up a perfect milk shake: banana flavor with two scoops of ice cream. But he'd forgotten to include a glass. It was only recently that he'd gotten used to his powers, begun to enjoy them.

So what would he do with them? Black magic or white magic? Good or evil?

He would leave that decision until later—at least until he'd passed his exams. And David was certain that he would pass. He was the seventh son of a seventh son. And he had never felt better in his life.